THROUGH THE DOLLS' HOUSE DOOR

OTHER YEARLING BOOKS YOU WILL ENJOY:

YEARLING BOOKS/YOUNG YEARLINGS/YEARLING CLASSICS are designed especially to entertain and enlighten young people. Patricia Reilly Giff, consultant to this series, received the bachelor's degree from Marymount College. She holds the master's degree in history from St. John's University, and a Professional Diploma in Reading from Hofstra University. She was a teacher and reading consultant for many years, and is the author of numerous books for young readers.

For a complete listing of all Yearling titles, write to Dell Readers Service, P.O. Box 1045, South Holland, IL 60473.

THROUGH THE DOLLS' HOUSE DOOR

JANE GARDAM

A Yearling Book

Published by
Dell Publishing
a division of
Bantam Doubleday Dell Publishing Group, Inc.
666 Fifth Avenue
New York, New York 10103

For Lucy, Tom and Jack

This work was first published in Great Britain in 1987 by Julia MacRae Books.

The trademark Yearling® is registered in the U.S. Patent and Trademark Office.

The trademark Dell® is registered in the U.S. Patent and Trademark Office.

ISBN: 0-440-40433-9

Reprinted by arrangement with William Morrow & Company, Inc., on behalf of Greenwillow Books

Printed in the United States of America

April 1991

10 9 8 7 6 5 4 3 2 1

OPM

Contents

1
Stuck

Claire put her head through the dolls' house door.

"Look," she said to Mary, "I've put my head through the dolls' house door."

Mary was making tea-parties for mice. "You can't," she said. "It's a small door."

"I've a small head."

Mary came down from the tea-party place on the cupboard top. She said, "Oh."

She said, "Goodness."

She said, "You have got your head stuck through the dolls' house door. It's a good thing there's no glass in the windows. You'd stuffocate."

"Suffocate," said Claire. "But I wouldn't. There's heaps of air and it's quite nice. My cheek is on a bed."

"Are you upstairs?"

"No. It's a sitting-room bed. The boys took the stairs."

The boys were Claire's brother and Mary's brother who were at school today. Claire and Mary were not at school because Claire had just had the mumps. The boys had finished the mumps. Mary was soon going to get the mumps. She was waiting for them. Claire's father had told her so. He was a doctor. He knew.

"Nothing to worry about," he said.

"No panic."

"Perfectly usual."

He said that about almost everything. Claire's mother didn't fuss, either, because she was a nurse. Today she had left Claire at Mary's house to play.

Claire and Mary played together almost every day, at school and at home. They set off to school together. They came home together. They had parties together. They had their hair cut together. They had their teeth looked at together. They went to Sunday School and dancing class together. They were very much like sisters.

"You couldn't have done it last week," said Mary, looking at Claire's body and legs sticking out of the dolls' house, "when you were all neck."

"You can't be *all* neck," said Claire.

"Snakes nearly are. Giraffes three-quarters are," said Mary. "You one quarter were. Your cheeks and neck were like a bear's, without fur."

"My neck's gone down, anyway," said Claire. "Like a puncture. I wish all of me could go down and be completely doll-size. Then I could have knocked on the door and walked in."

"The knocker's gone," said Mary. "The boys took it for a weapon."

"It was no bigger than a salt-spoon," said Claire. "A spoon for a fly. Or a beetle. It was the right size for a Trojan soldier."

"The soldiers had a battle," said Mary. "Upstairs. As soon as one gets killed the boys drop him through the hole. That's why the boys took the stairs out. For dropping."

"I think a soldier must have fallen on the bed," said Claire. "Under my cheek is prickling."

"Can you see the dolls?"

"I can see Sigger. And Miss Bossy, a bit. I can't see Small Cry. The prickle under my cheek is hurting."

"Wiggle your cheek."

"Cheeks don't wiggle."

"Wiggle the whole of your head. Rub it about on the eiderdown."

"That's better," said Claire. "He's somewhere in my hair now."

4

"Why not wiggle your head out of the doorway again?"

"No. It's nice in here. I'm looking right in at the dolls' house dolls' house."

This was a needle-box that Claire's mother had made into a dolls' house for the dolls' dolls.

So the needle-box dolls' house stood in the dolls' house.

And the dolls' house stood in Mary's house.

One, two, three, like a seed in a pod on a tree in a forest.

Claire had wanted Mary's mother to make a smaller dolls' house still, to put inside the needle-box for the needle-box dolls to play with. And then an even smaller . . . And then a smaller . . . But Mary had said, "No. Stop. We'll get dizzy."

"Hot in here," said Miss Bossy. "And dark."

"Don't speak of it," wailed Small Cry. "Let us cloooooose our eyes and pray."

"It's quite interesting," said Sigger. "It's just a different sort of morning. And it won't last for ever."

"Oh COME ON, Claire," said Mary. "Pull your silly head out and have some tea on the cupboard."

"Not yet."

"There's coca-cola cake and jelly-sprats and chocolate-lettuce."

No answer.

"There's jelly-chips."

"Uck."

"They're magic chips. They're made of silver ice-cream. In icicles."

"Oh, all right then," and Claire tried to pull out her head.

"It's stuck," she said.

"It can't be. It went in."

"It's changed shape. My chin's grown. Or the mumps have come back."

"Shall I pull on your feet?"

"No."

"I'll go and get some magic to sprinkle."

"Or get your Mummy," said Claire.

"Yes."

Mary went to get the magic and Claire went to sleep.

"Well, this is a fine bag of sausages," said Miss Bossy. "The house is as full as an egg." She was a large doll and was compressed tightly into the sitting-room, her head against the ceiling and her feet in the needle-box. She was very old and wooden, with hinges in her arms and legs and red painted circles on her cheeks and black painted curves for her hair, neatly finished with a round black ring painted on the back of her neck, but you couldn't see that.

"Cry? Cry?" she called. "Small Cry? Where are you?"

"The other side," called Cry – or wept Cry. She was a little miserable doll who wore a raggedy shawl and one shoe. When she had arrived in the house as a Christmas present long ago she had been dressed in sticking-out white net and stars. Almost at once the net had grown shabby and torn and been thrown away and Small Cry had become used only for dressing-up. Sometimes she was a witch and sometimes she was a space-traveller and sometimes she was the Lord Mayor of London or the Queen. She didn't know where she was or who she was from one day to the next. She liked life only on the days when the children took her from the dolls' house and set her in a boat on the water of Mary's blue plastic paddling-pool in the garden. The boys particularly tipped and squeezed the sides of the pool about until she fell out of the boat and there had to be a rescue. They shrieked and rescued, rescued and shrieked, as if she were a valuable doll.

"Cry, Cry," shouted Miss Bossy again. "What has happened to Sigger?"

"Oh, *she'll* be all right," mourned Cry.

"*I'm* all right," called cheerful Sigger.

(She was always all right.) "I'm lying flat. I'm under the bed. It's a bit saggy."

"I'm more worried about the General," said Cry.

"It's not the General!"

"Yes. She's squashed him. That stupid Claire's squashed him. He's under her cheek. Dead, of course."

"Snuffle, squffle, puffle," said something under Claire's head and a fierce grey plastic face, the size of a baby's finger-nail, looked out from beside a yellow hair-ribbon. A grey, plastic shield began to wave beside Claire's ear. It was the size of a quarter of one of Claire's eyelids, which were closed. "Trojans don't die," cried the soldier, "they fall nobly in battle. Help!!!!" and he went slithering down Claire's left-side bunch of hair, like somebody just learning to ski. He was left hanging like mad on to the tail-end of the bunch with his legs all desperate and wagging about.

Claire in her sleep gave a sigh and turned her face round on to the bed so that her nose made the mattress more saggy still and Sigger had to breathe out. Then she turned her face up the other side and the soldier, hanging on to the hair, was dragged underneath her head again.

"That's done it," said Cry. "Can't you do something, Bossy? It's all up. End of the story. Amen and goodbye. He's dead this time all right. Suffocated-stuffocated."

"He's not," called Sigger from the saggy dark. "He's heaving himself about. I can see a little wriggle going along the bottom of the mattress. There he goes!"

"Gaaaaaaarh," groaned the Trojan, squeezing out from between cheek and bed and skirting the right-hand hair bunch. He collapsed against Claire's mouth which was like a lilo cushion. Her breath came softly down her nostrils in a cool blast, like air-conditioning. "Earthquake," roared the soldier. "Serious earthquake. Number 999 on the Richter scale. Natural disaster."

"Earthquake, twaddle," said Miss Bossy. "It's urban disgrace. Case of serious over-crowding. Poverty-line. Authorities. Scandal. Day-and-Age. Band-aid. We'll have to speak to her at this rate. Great head filling up our one state drawing-room."

"Or speak to that Mary," said Cry.

"Yes, where's that Mary?"

"Oh, *she's* gone. Downstairs to the mother. She doesn't care," said Cry. "Nobody cares, come to that. We're only good for throwing about and bundling away now. Once we were loved. I don't know why we were born."

"Can I come out now?" asked Sigger. "I want to see her face close up."

"Nothing exciting there," said Cry.

"She's not as ugly as she was last week," said Bossy.

"Poor thing," said Sigger, peering close, "how awful to be huge. Even without the mumps. Just human-huge. However does she manage to get about?"

"She doesn't," said Cry. "She gets stuck."

"I think I've got my foot caught in the needle-box," said Bossy. "There's a bit of a commotion going on in there, too. There's trouble wherever you look these days. I can feel it in my big toe. Like rain coming."

"I expect it's only the needles," said Sigger. "It's a good job we aren't humans or we'd all have suffocated-stuffocated by now. Aren't we lucky to be dolls?"

8

(Down in the needle-box a Crewel-darner Number Three hissed at a steel bodkin that he was glad to be a needle.)

"*Suffocate*," said Bossy. "Let's get it right. It's a human word we've learned, so we'd better hang on to it. Well, of course Claire was always very silly."

"But she's nice," said Sigger, "and she'd be very pretty if she wasn't huge."

"She's got lovely yellow hair-ribbons," said Cry. "They'd make a beautiful dress. Not that anyone'd bother to make a dress for me."

"Hello Mary," said her mother in the sunny kitchen. It was a hot day. All the doors and windows were open. The garden outside looked cool and green and flowery and the water in the paddling-pool was flashing blue.

"Why ever don't you and Claire come down and play in the garden? Stifling in that stuffy roof."

"Claire's in the dolls' house."

"Oh I see. Did she knock on the door and walk in?"

"The door-knocker's come off. It's a sword now for a Trojan. She just pushed open the door –"

"– and walked in?" Mary's mother handed her a peppermint cream from a painted tin with camels on it. She joined in games. "Cut this up for the dolls. It's a snow cake. I expect they're hot and hungry."

"They're a bit squashed today," said Mary, "with Claire in there."

"She'd have to shrink very small to get in the dolls' house," said her mother. "Down to the size of Miss Bossy at least. And Miss Bossy is really too big."

"You can't prune her," said Mary, "like plants."

"Of course not. I mean that she's a bit big to be a dolls'

9

house doll. When she was my doll, when I was five, she sat in style on the nursery shelf. There was something very wonderful about her, everyone said. Some sort of history. I can't remember. I'd almost forgotten her. Is Claire going to stay small for ever? Shall we have to carry her in our pockets?"

"No. She's no smaller at all," said Mary. "Well, a bit smaller than last week, that's all."

"Yes, her neck. Quite gone now. All quite comfortable again."

"She's not comfortable," said Mary.

"Quite gone," said her mother. "No panic. Nothing to fuss about, as her father says," and she started to make lemonade out of six lemons and some sugar. The sugar was kept in a pot the shape of a cat. She took off its head and poured half a cat-ful into a bowl. She added some crystals from two little packets.

The crystals reminded Mary that she had been on her way to get magic to help Claire out of the dolls' house.

"I'm just going for some magic," she said.

"*That's* right."

"To help Claire to get out of the dolls' house."

"*That's* right." (Mary's mother got dreamy when she was cooking.) "Let me know if I can help."

"She wants to see you," said Mary. "Could you come?"

"In a minute," said her mother, grating lemon rinds.

"Stick the door-knocker into the tight bit of the hair to help you up," said Miss Bossy. "Quick-sharp now. Look lively."

"Don't you start telling the Military how to behave," said the soldier. "Madam. I'm Trojan Hero First Class. Plus Bar. Plus Star and Garter. Knight of the Golden Fleece, return journey, though that was a bit before my time. I'm trained to

10

take time and not cut corners. I was through Troy you know. *Oh*, yes. Whole campaign. Did the Odyssey. Well, it's hard to settle down after a war."

"You'll never reach the hair-ribbon if you don't hurry," said Bossy, "never mind Odysseys."

"Odds I do," said the Trojan soldier, but dolls are poor at puns and only sweet Sigger smiled. "I'll go at the proper pace," said the soldier, "that's what I'm saying," and he plunged the door-knocker into Claire's fat plait, below the ribbon and the elastic band. Claire sighed in her sleep.

"Oh, ah," wailed Cry, "he'll never do it. She's waking up."

"I'm not at all sure I want to do it," said the Trojan. "Ribbon-stealing. Good heavens. What have I come to? Trojans don't pillage."

"What's pillage?"

"Loot."

"What's loot?" asked Sigger.

"I can play the lute," said Cry and began to sing a dreary, twangy song.

"Stop making poor jokes," said Bossy, "and let me think. I've got the whole foot stuck in the needle-box now and something's pricking my ankle hinge."

"There," said the Trojan, standing proudly alongside the hair-ribbon. "Here we are. I'll ease it loose with the door-knocker. Sword, they call it. Sword my foot!"

"No, sword *my* foot," said Bossy.

"Here we go. I'm getting it. It's just a question of Science."

"Never mind Science," said Cry, "I want a new dress."

The soldier eased the door-knocker into the tight part of the bow. "Tricky," he said. "It's all snarled up with the elastic-band! I once heard an elastic-band. Lovely snappy tunes you get in an elastic-band." (This time Miss Bossy kept a poker face. She touched her hair sniffily especially the black circle at the back.)

"One good pun deserves another," said Sigger, trying to be pleasant. Miss Bossy looked down her nose.

"Fancy having elastic-bands in hair," said mouldy Cry. "That mother, the nurse, is hopeless. Splits the ends. It'll all fall out, silly woman."

"Yours has fallen out without elastic-bands," said Bossy.

"That is my tragedy," said Cry, drooping her face towards the carpet, "and the cruelty of fate. The boys cut it off at a whim. They don't seem to know that I'm a female. And refined," and she looked at her painted finger-nails that were all that were left of the days when she had been a princess in net.

"Here we go," cried the soldier. "Stand clear. Timber, etc."

"Timber, fiddle-sticks," said Bossy.

"Timber is fiddle-sticks," said Cry. "At least fiddle-sticks are timber."

"They're nothing of the sort, they're made of cats' insides," said Bossy. "Be accurate. It's ribbon we're capturing, not a tree. Here – if I lean forward just a little. Like this. I think I can – just catch – Ha! There! Very pretty indeed. It will make a perfectly splendid dress, Cry. It will even perhaps cheer you up. It will suit you down to the ground."

"I want it short," said Cry, never satisfied.

"I'll roll it up neatly and put it away," said Bossy.

"Can I have the other ribbon, too?" asked Cry. "It's just out of sight. Under her head."

"We *could* try to make her turn her head again," said the Trojan, tired, but ready to endure to the end.

12

"She's really very sound asleep," said Sigger who had crawled from under the bed and was looking very interestedly up Claire's nose. "There are lots of little gold threads up there," she said. "Beautifully arranged. And her eyes have long, curled-back black threads all along the edges of the eye-covers. Very silky. Whoops!"

Claire sighed and Sigger hung on tightly to the end of the bed to stop being blown away. "She's been eating radishes," she said, "out of Mary's garden, like they do. With all the soil on. She must be better. All through the mumps it was only ice-cream. Oh – look at the black threads. They're moving."

Claire's eye, the one nearest the bed, tried to open, but it was only a slit. The top eye did better. A gleamy, bulgy circle of blue and black lines drawn very close together appeared, and in the middle of them a black blob. It looked like a flower except that, unlike a flower, Sigger could see her own face in the black blob. She thought, "My face looks like a small Claire-face. I wonder if I'm really –" but then she got muddled. The cover with the fringe along its edge dropped over the bright wet looking-glass flower again.

"How frightful," said Small Cry, peeping. "Quite gross and disgusting. It is The Human Eye."

"Just Science," said the Trojan soldier, gazing. "We are fearfully and wonderfully made – at least they are. It's human mechanics – skin-flap with polished wires, concave below. Functional. To do with dust and grit getting in. And of course tears."

The dolls sat for a while pondering the mystery of tears.

"Nothing unpleasant," said the Trojan.

"Wonderfully beautiful," said Sigger.

"What's beauty?" said the Trojan. "By the time you've decided, you're dead. Give me action. Here we go," and very cleverly and bravely, because of his hard military training, he climbed the dome of slippery silk that was Claire's head, for the second time. "Like walking on ice," he said, "oily, polished ice. Proper assault-course. They keep her well-shampooed. 'Shout from the trench, Achilles' – Whoop-la! I'll just drop down in to the parting."

Holding tight with one hand to the elastic-band, he straddled his feet, steadied himself on the steep slope and began to work away at the second ribbon with the door-knocker.

Mary in the garden picked poppy-heads.

She opened their round seed-boxes and gathered up the seeds. She put the shiny black coal-splinter seeds on a leaf and took them to the kitchen.

"First magic," she said.

"That's a good girl," said her mother.

She went back and picked seven velvet snap-dragon flowers: dark crimson, rhubarb-pink, hair-ribbon yellow, white.

She took them to the kitchen.

"Second magic," she said.

She went back in to the garden and picked three purple pansies, one geranium leaf and a sprig of blue plumbago.

"Plumbago magic," she said.

"Plumbago is a very *painful* flower," said her mother who made these small jokes. "Claire is very quiet."

"Yes. She's got her head stuck in the dolls' house door," said Mary.

"*I* see," said her mother, pouring boiling water over the sugar and lemons and crystals. She began to stir it heavily, slowly, trying to make the sugar melt, round and round with a strong wooden spoon. Mary went into the warm garden to the vegetable patch and picked nine big gooseberries: four green, hard ones that needed a shave, three pale-pink squelchy ones like flesh, and two miserable white ones that had spent their life deep under the bush, their tufts brushing the ground. They had never seen the sun. They reminded her of Small Cry's face. Poor Small Cry. She had been pretty once. Perhaps they ought to be kinder to Small Cry.

Mary sat on the grass and arranged the gooseberries in a row. Four lots of magic now, she thought. It ought to be enough to get Claire out.

"MARY!"

"Yes?"
She went running.

Her mother stood on the step of the kitchen door, the strong wooden spoon on high like a Trojan's door-knocker.

"WHAT did you say?"
"WHAT did you say?"

"Magic," said Mary. "Magic to get Claire out. She's stuck in the dolls' house. Her head's stuck. She's quite all right. She's very very quiet. I told you. I told you. She's got her head stuck in the dolls' house door."

"There," said Miss Bossy, "a nice length of top quality yellow ribbon neatly folded. Where shall we put it? Thank the General nicely, Cry."

"Thanks," said Cry dolefully. "I don't expect anything will come of it. I'm the victim type. Rags for life, that's me. But thanks all the same."

"All in the course of duty," said the Trojan. He was sitting exhaustedly on Claire's nose. "My word, I've had adventures in my time, but ribbons off the heads of girl-giants! I

15

might make use of one I suppose – fling it up through the stairwell and get them to catch on. Then leg-over-leg as the dog went to Dover. Rejoin my unit."

("What's he on about?" asked some of the needles and pins. "Dover?")

"I'll stow them in the needle-box house," said Miss Bossy. "Leaning forward to grab them has eased my wooden ankle-hinge. I can lift my foot now."

"Let us consider," said the Trojan, and put an armoured and greaved leg on either side of Claire's nose and dug in his heels.

"Oh don't," said Sigger, "you'll scratch her. Oh, Trojan, Trojan – do look out! And oh – whatever's all that noise outside?"

"Footsteps pounding," said Miss Bossy.

"We have reached our end," Cry cried, wringing her painted nails, and Bossy with a quick, cunning shove pushed the ribbon-roll into the needle-box with her foot, and shut the lid on all the squeaks and lamentations and gasping bad-tempered fuss that needle-box Creatures make.

"No panic."

"Perfectly usual."

"Nothing to worry about," came the sound of Claire's father the doctor. He had just called to take Claire home and had bumped into Mary and her mother on the stairs. Mary's mother was all lemonade and screams.

"No panic – " but his kind voice stopped when he saw Claire's feet and Claire's legs and Claire's body and Claire's neck and nothing on the end of it except the dolls' house.

And everything was quite, quite still.

"Perfectly usual," he said, but now in a very trembly way, and Mary's mother gave such a piercing shriek that all the dolls had headaches for days.

And inside the dolls' house Claire's nose with the soldier's feet digging in to it began to crinkle up.

And to wrinkle up.

Up. Up.

Up.

And her eye-covers with the wires attached began to squeeze up and to wrinkle up.

To crinkle, crinkle up.

Wrinkle up.

And her sleeping mouth began to open up. Open. Open. Wider, Wider.

There was a very urgent scrabbling of human hands at the side-fastening of the dolls' house and then Miss Bossy said, "Hold tight. Hold tight all of you," and before the whole front of the house could be eased loose –

ATTISHOO!!

and Claire's head shot back out of the dolls' house door, quite safely attached to the rest of her.

"But I *told* you," said Mary in the bath, later, "I told you. I kept on telling you."

"How *could* you! How *could* you. Just go out playing in the garden. She might have – Oh Mary! – suffocated. Oh Mary, Mary."

"There are no windows. No glass in the windows. She couldn't have suffocated. Anyway she was happy."

"Happy!"

"Enjoying it."

"Enjoying – I never heard!"

"And," said Mary, tears falling on the bath-water with plops, "my neck aches. Her neck doesn't ache and she's the one who's being fussed. I'm just being scolded and blamed and my neck aches."

"*Your* neck –" said her mother. "*Your* neck? I don't see why *your* neck should – Oh dear! Oh goodness! Oh yes of course! I do. Of course. Oh poor old Mary, yes. It will. It may. It's the mumps."

She felt Mary's neck, "Oh yes – it's the good old mumps all right."

"Nothing to fuss about. No panic," snuffled Mary, very pleased to be cuddled and put to bed and told there'd be a story. "Nothing un-usual."

"I expect you were full of the mumps when you came down to the kitchen," said her mother. "You'd gone all silly and dreamy with the mumps."

"*I'd* gone all silly and dreamy –" said Mary, amazed.

"Yes – *poor* Mary," said her mother, "yes, that's what it was."

In another bath next door Claire was being told how silly she had been, too. "You might have had to be *sawn* out," said her father, "and then where would the dolls' house have been?"

"It's almost not there already," said Claire. "It's awful. An awful ugly dolls' house. No stairs. No windows. And they're not a bit happy in there. Any of them. Those dolls."

"I'll do something about it," he said. "I've been meaning to. New staircase. Glue up the front door."

"And make a separate place for the soldiers. Would Mary's mummy let you?"

"Yes."

"And her own bed for Small Cry? Instead of the fireplace?"

"Yes, we'll smarten up the dolls a bit."

"Sigger doesn't need it. She's always happy. And Miss Bossy doesn't need it. She's happy as long as she can boss. It's poor Cry who's in a state. She's so awful."

"We'll try and do something for Cry. Goodness – what's that?"

A Trojan soldier had fallen out of Claire's hair into the bath. They watched him slowly, slowly drop down through the water, very dignified, not twitching a muscle. Claire scooped him out and stood him by the taps. "He's had a hard day," she said.

Her father went to fetch a dry towel and Claire looked eye to eye at the Trojan who held his shield bravely and looked eye to eye back at her.

"Thank you," she said.

"Oh I enjoyed it," he replied. "An interesting afternoon. We lack activity in there. Very much worth it."

"And Cry's going to have a lovely new dress," said Claire. Then she thought, However did I know that?

2
Scatter

It was Easter time. Daffodils tapped their buds and tossed their flowers against the dolls' house where it stood in the wet grass at the end of the garden.

It was early morning and it was going to be a breezy, showery day.

All around in the daffodils and across the lawn the dolls lay scattered as if there had been some frightful explosion. There was a trail of them from the dolls' house door to the gate in the hedge. The hedge divided Mary's house from Claire's house, but only just. It was very flimsy, more of a cobweb than a hedge. Even inside, Mary's house was only just divided from Claire's, for there was a door on the landing which was very often open. Only when the boys had really roaring quarrels was the door bolted across for punishment.

The daffodil patch stretched across the end of both gardens where the cobweb hedge faded out and behind the daffodils the garden became a small wood where there would soon be bluebells. It was a lovely place. In the two silent, early-morning houses the daffodils swung their trumpets about but wakened nobody. All curtains were drawn and all was quiet.

Then Claire's mother came out of her garden door and walked slowly in her dressing-gown and bare feet until she reached the dolls' house. In a minute Mary's mother came out of her kitchen door and joined her. Together they began to stoop and pick up the toys and dolls from yesterday's games, talking quietly, wandering about.

Then a sleepy shout came out of Mary's house and a scruffly, half-awake person, who was Mary's father in orange pyjamas and up-on-end black hair, looked out to say that there was some tea. Next, a neat person in a short, smart tomato-coloured dressing-gown and flamingo legs, who was Claire's father, the doctor, came out of his house and said, "Ah, tea."

Everybody walked towards the tea, and as they reached Mary's kitchen the two mothers propped some of the dolls they had gathered along the kitchen window-sill above the dustbins. The shining doll, Sigger, went inside with them however, and settled on the working-surface beside the great white sugar-pot Cat. There all the Creatures stayed all day long until it was dark again and the daffodils had stopped swinging and the wind had died down and it was night.

"It will be a matter of seconds," said miserable Cry in the darkness (Creatures speak better in darkness), "of *seconds* before I fall in this dustbin and am lost for ever. Not that anyone will care."

"Pish," replied the Dutch doll, Miss Bossy. "Pish."

"I am *so* delicate, *so* light and frail. It is my aristocratic background. Look at my high insteps. The least breath of wind will do for me. My second name is Thistledown."

"Thistledown Cry," said Miss Bossy. "Whatever next!"

"Oh, but I sympathise," said a huge, bulging doll called Plum. "I have the tenderest of constitutions, too." She had fat pink legs and pink cheeks rounded up in a permanent gleaming smile. Her hair was spangly marmalade gold and she was covered in plum-coloured velvet with satiny frills and bows. She was Claire's doll, and newish. When she had arrived as a Christmas present everyone had said "Oooh" and "Aaah" and "How wonderful", and Plum had grinned out at the world and been arranged on Claire's bed with her skirts spread out.

Yet you could somehow see she wasn't going to fit in.

Quite soon she had been taken off somewhere through the cobweb hedge by the dog. Later she had been laid out along the top floor of the dolls' house and its door shut on her for peace of mind. She had filled up the whole accommodation of the top floor, which was of course the garrison, and caused the soldiers such discomfort that they had begun to drop each other through all the cracks and fling themselves down the fine new matchbox staircase in showers. They were all put in a plastic bag in the end and stuffed down the chimney.

"And I should think so, too," Plum had said to the ceiling, smirking. She was not an easy doll. She looked so very perfect that nobody knew what to say to her. She had not enjoyed the night before, lying out in the wet grass. "Goodness knows what game those boys thought they were playing," she said now to Miss Bossy.

"Human rockets."

"But we're not humans," said Cry.

"It's just as well. If we were we would be dead."

"They were just trying to make us fly," said Sigger through the glass. "It's a way they have."

"Flinging things about," said Plum, "like savages." She had not heard Sigger. She was a little deaf and it was anyway difficult to hear Sigger's light voice through the glass. Sigger was speaking it seemed a little quietly these days and looking slightly faded. Lonely without her friends far away on the window-sill, she still remained cheerful and happy. All day she watched what had happened in the kitchen, contentedly, wondering a little at the serious talk, the wrinkling of foreheads as the fathers and mothers drank tea and discussed. The feeling in the kitchen was curious, she thought. Uncertain.

By the third afternoon something seemed to have been decided. The mothers and fathers began to move briskly about. They looked excited and Sigger listened as carefully as she could, squeezing her eyes, holding her breath (Sigger of all the Creatures was the one with breath), and wishing above all things that she spoke the human language. She could understand certain words – names, commands, events – "Claire" or "Hurry" or "Dinner-time", but most of it was very foreign. "A foreign tongue," Miss Bossy called it, but in fact it was just a tongue. Sigger and the other creatures spoke without tongues, by silent vibrations like the stars.

"Didn't you *Know*?" enquired a voice in her ear but above her head. "Do I understand you have not *Heard*?"

It was the voice of the China Cat, the noble being she leaned upon, twanging through his china side. He was not attempting to look at her but straight ahead and high above her, painted whiskers spiked. He was a magnificent animal and could hold a full two pounds of sugar. His white china coat had an expensive, bluish tinge and was painted all over at intervals with bunches of cherries, one, two, or three to a bunch. His eyes were green and princely and he seldom talked to dolls. Sigger felt very honoured to be in conversation with him.

"We live down in the daffodil patch," she said. "We don't hear very much. Our house is the old dolls' house."

"I know of it," said the Cat. "Some years ago I observed it being carried out for cleaning."

"We used to live right up in the loft," said Sigger. "We weren't exactly at the hub of things there either, but we were very comfortable, really."

"Mixed lot, aren't you?" said the Cat. "Rooming house? Tenement? Multi-racial?"

"Oh yes. And visible and invisible. It was very interesting."

26

"Personally I like to be with my own sort. With creatures like myself."

Sigger looked all round for more cats painted with bunches of cherries, which she might have missed. She hadn't noticed any in the kitchen before and she didn't now. There was the living cat of course, asleep on the warm patch of floor where the central heating pipe passed below. This cat was tightly curled like a snail almost standing on its head – a ruffian of a cat who had one day come in out of the cold and not got round to leaving: an easy-come, easy-go, un-interested cat, without love or curiosity.

"No relation," said the China Cat. "My relatives are very dispersed, I'm afraid. Very far-flung."

"We're far-flung, too," said Sigger. "They're always flinging us about. Long ago they decided to do the dolls' house up for us. After that time Claire nearly beheaded herself, they put in a staircase and dabbed about with lovely patches of wallpaper. When we got shabby again they took us all out into the garden for a good scrub. But then they forgot us."

"Typical," said the Cat. "But there is worse for you ahead."

"Worse?"

"Yes. They have come to a decision."

"Decision?"

"The mothers and fathers. These adult humans are always making decisions, most of them unnecessary. It is the most irrational thing about them. They can't let be."

"What – ?"

But then the light was switched on and Mary's father came crashing in to make yet more tea. He took the Cat's head off for sugar and forgot to put it back. He dropped the teapot lid and churned his hands about in his hair, and groaned.

Mary's brother came in. "What's the *matter*," he said. "It's midnight."

"Nothing. Couldn't sleep. Oh Lor'."

"You've spilt the milk."

"I'm thinking. Why are you awake, Tim?"

"I couldn't sleep. I'm thinking. What's the matter?"

"What?" His father scattered biscuits about the floor and the furry snail shuddered and shook itself and got up and stalked away. It stood looking hard at the back door until Tim unlocked and opened it for him.

"Nothing's the matter. Go back to bed."

When the kitchen was empty again Sigger said, "*What* will be worse, Cat?" but the Cat could not vibrate without its head and she had to wait until the following afternoon.

Then the Cat said, "They are all going away. They are going away for ever."

Sigger jumped. She had been dreaming, watching all day the flicker of the silver birches out of the window beyond the backs of the dolls' heads on the window-ledge.

"Going away?"

"Going away," said the Cat. "All of them. Claire's family, Mary's family, *in toto*."

"What is *toto*?"

"Two fathers," said the Cat, "two mothers, two brothers, two girls. Even the fishes in that fish tank. Even, I wouldn't wonder, that object, that hearth-rug, that walking flea-forest."

"Even the dolls and the Creatures?" said Sigger. "Oh but how nice. We shall all enjoy a journey – except of course for Small Cry. Small Cry suffers from an awful illness called misery."

"May we change the subject?" asked the Cat. "I have heard of Small Cry. Isn't she that grey little heap above the dustbins, rather reminiscent of a dying dishcloth?"

"Oh but that's her yellow dress," said Sigger. "It used to be beautiful. But, dear Cat, please tell me, is the going-away to be for dolls?"

"Who can say about dolls?" said the Cat. "Who can say about cats, come to that."

"But of course they'll take you," said Sigger, "you're so wonderful."

The Cat vibrated.

"And so useful. Holding all that sugar. They couldn't live without you."

"Sugar's not as popular as it used to be," said the Cat. "It would be easier to carry in a bag. They could just empty me out and throw me away. I don't travel easily. I have to be stuffed and wrapped. Like vine-leaves."

"You're as doleful as Cry," said Sigger. "I hope she's not getting to an infectious stage. I've wondered before about that. She can't get at Miss Bossy, but the Trojan was the sort that catches things and so is Plum. Sometimes I wonder if that's why the Trojan disappeared."

"Ah," said the Cat, and someone came along and removed his head again and it was next Tuesday week before he could add, "Disappeared? Alas."

"Yes – I liked him," said Sigger.

"I meant disappeared in the general."

"Yes, he was the General."

"I *mean*," said the Cat with a gleam of princely annoyance very imperiously disguised, "I mean that disappearance is the terrible, frightening thing -- the disappearance of the pattern around us. Think of the things that have disappeared in this house – beads and balls and scissors and toys and ribbons. Nobody notices. They are not really important. So they vanish. Remember that fuss once about yellow hair-ribbons? Vanished. As we shall all vanish in the end. Sawdust to sawdust."

"Oh but they don't vanish. That's not Scientific, Cat. They're all here somewhere. Those hair-ribbons became Cry's dress. The soldier brought them back from a great journey. A journey over mountains and hills, of gazing into dark tunnels and rose-pink mazes, of climbing a ravine between banks of impenetrable sprouting vegetation. Called Hair. And of being blown away at last by a typhoon. Of course it was all Claire's head, really. Whatever *really* means."

"Killed him, did it? Blotted him out? No trace? Disappeared?"

"Well, we never saw the General again after he was whirled into the air. He'd had time to throw the yellow ribbons to Miss Bossy. He was very efficient. Then he was gone. Afterwards Cry sewed them up into a dress. She's good at sewing though she does get it all over tears."

"Each one of us shall soon be all over tears," said the Cat, glaring at space, and he refused to say one word more. Sigger leaned against him respectfully, wondering how she could get the tremendous news of their departing out through the glass to the window-sill above the dustbins, how she could get a message down the garden to the chimneyful of soldiers.

Many days passed.

Plum fell into the dustbin on one of them when a lid had been left off. She was carted away unnoticed.

Many days passed.

The easy-come furry family cat got grumpier than ever as the house became frantic with activity and furniture began

30

to be stacked up in heaps. One night it walked out and never came back indoors again.

And many days passed.

Many days passed and Sigger was moved about from the kitchen work-top beside the Cat, to the shelf above it, beside the jam thermometer, then to the top of the bread-bin, then, very dangerously, to the edge of the sink, then back again across the kitchen where for some time she hung head-downward between the glass of the fish-tank and the glass of the window. She was facing the fish-tank and the fish opened and shut their inside-out mouths at her and their faces looked horrified.

"Don't look horrified," said Sigger to them, upside down. "They won't leave you behind. It would be cruelty to animals." The China Cat vibrated with a shudder, then froze back into its pretence of being a statue, noble and ready for death.

The fish continued to look agonised, butting around the tank and swirling their milky tails.

And many days passed.

3
Lost

Summer came.

Silence came.

An empty house. No people.

But that was nothing for the two families always went away together for the summer holidays. Long ago the dolls and Creatures had all gone with them, but lately only one or other of them had been chosen. The children were growing older now and needed fewer toys. Claire still loved Miss Bossy, and Mary, who was motherly, loved Cry because Cry looked all the time as if she needed someone, but the boys now hated Cry, stuck pins in her and did operations on her and flung her into the sea, where she fell splat on the waves and was scooped out on the tide before being tossed roly-poly back with a face like a wet blanket, which was what poor Cry was.

Terrible things happened to Cry, or nearly happened. She was the sort who trembled and groaned so much that there was never really time for any complete happening, bad or good. Adventures of all kinds hurried away from Cry and attached themselves to less grumbling sorts of creatures, saying, "My word, that last one was a mope."

Sigger was motherly, too – Sigger head-down behind the fish-tank. *Tap*, *tap*, she went with her heels on the glass of the window behind her. *Tap*, *tap*. "Cry? Miss Bossy? Are you all right out there?" She called at night, for speech and movement come more easily to Creatures at night. She could just see the flat black egg-shape of Bossy's wooden head.

"Where's Plum?" she heard Miss Bossy call – the cleaning lady, Mrs Grudgely, had left the window slightly open by mistake.

"I think she must have dropped off. Or perhaps they took her."

"*Took* her," came Bossy's voice. "Took *her*. Good gracious, all that satin and spangle on the sands."

"I suppose it was her turn," said Sigger. "We've all been taken in our time. I suppose it's because she's new."

"She'll be impossible when she comes back," said Bossy. "She'll need putting in her place."

"They'll have done that," said Cry from down behind the dustbin where she had now fallen. "Those boys will have put her in an open boat by now. They're savages to dolls. I was once nearly swept out to China."

"China's not near Wales," said Bossy.

"Yes it is," said Cry. "Ask the Cat. He's Welsh. Welsh China. It says so on his underneath. I saw it when I lived on the draining-board once. They were washing him out."

Sigger looked up nervously at the Cat and thought of apologising for Cry being such a fool, but noticed then that there was in fact something rather Chinese – certainly foreign – about the Cat's eyes and the set of his whiskers. He had first arrived among them while they were in Wales one holiday long ago. He had been bought at the gift shop in Tenby.

She began to think drowsily of Tenby. The dusty sun struck into the kitchen. All that summer it shone, so hot, so splendid. How delicious it would be for them all to be near the great green breakers and the small crabby pools, the limpets and the sand-castles, the buckets-and-spades of Wales.

Perhaps Wales *had* something to do with China. She would like to have asked the Cat outright but he was in one of his remote moods at present. He did not *seem* Welsh. One had not even heard him sing, for example, or take an interest in Rugby football on the kitchen telly. "Do you ever feel like a sing, Cat?" she asked after brooding and dozing and imagining the salty breezes and the white sands and the towering black cliffs for several days. But the Cat did not reply.

Sigger thought how she would like a conversation. Or a story. A story of high adventure. She thought of the days when the Trojan would tell tales of his wonderful life.

One morning the cleaning lady arrived and took the Cat's head off.

Of course she took his head off every time she came to Mary's house because she needed four teaspoonsful out of him for her first cup of tea – hers and the milkman's. Twice a week she visited Claire's house through the summer holidays to see that everything was all right and to dust about and arrange flowers in the windows to make the house feel it was still alive when the family was away, and to keep away burglars. Then she came on to Mary's house and did the same. There wasn't much cleaning to do, with everyone in Wales, so she would open the door to the milkman, ease off her shoes and sit chatting with him until her kettle boiled. Sometimes she brought her little boy, who was fat like a grub, and sat him on the work-top. When he kept touching things – he liked bright, glittery things – she said, "That'll do," and handed him a biscuit. He was a good boy. He sat still as the China Cat.

When the kettle boiled Mrs Grudgely didn't move either. She leaned back with a waving arm, poured water into the teapot, swirled it round and trickled it into the sink. Then she stretched for the tea-bags, dropped them at arm's length into the pot, filled it up, and began to eat biscuits, crunch-crunch, dribble of crumbs, in a chorus with the milkman and her child. When the tea was ready, she poured it out and leaned back again and lifted off the Cat's head to dig her spoon into him.

"Yes, moving," said Ma Grudgely. "That's what they're planning. That'll do, Chetwode."

"I'll be sorry," said the milkman. "Nice people. They make an interest."

"Oh, they're nice enough," said the cleaning lady. "That'll do, Chatty."

Chetwode is a funny name for a baby and so it was shortened to Chatty, but that was even sillier because the baby wasn't chatty at all. He hardly said one word and you could see he'd always be the same. He was thoughtful. He might have been the Cat's kitten.

"Oh, they're nice enough. But they're very cluttery. Live in a mess. Now me, I like things put away." She leaned to the Cat and spooned out more sugar, nearly sweeping his head to the floor. "Well, we'd better be getting off," she said later. Not bothering to do much to the dirty tea mugs, she shouldered Chatty and went, followed by the kind milkman who tried all the door handles and twisted the taps tight in case of drips. "I don't like a house empty like this," he said. "Feels dead. Full of dead things."

He's right, thought upside-down Sigger watching the endlessly weaving fish. When it got to bedtime the fish propped themselves up against the sides of the tank for a sleep, which made things stiller than ever.

Not that the fish ever talked to her when they were awake. "Cat," she called, "Cat?"

But china cats can't vibrate with their heads off. The real cat was sitting outside, sulking, with his back to the house and full of hunting thoughts.

"I've something of a notion," said Mrs Grudgely one day, removing Chatty's fingers from the fish-tank where the fish were pop-eyed with fury, "I've a notion that they're not coming back."

"What, this family?" said the milkman.

"Neither family. That'll do. Just look what he's got. Box full of pins. One of them in your mouth, me lad, and it's doctors and clanging bells."

Chatty had found the needle-box that used to be the dolls' dolls' house. It had been brought in from the garden during the tidying up of the Creatures, with odd bits and bobs of dolls' house furniture, the morning when the four parents had so solemnly talked. Chatty liked its glittery top. It was a smooth black box the size of a biscuit and set in the lid was a border of shining blue, pink and silver flakes. In the centre of the lid was a bright little knob of glass. Chatty had a chew at the knob.

"Give it here. He's a funny one is Chat. Mad on things that shine. Like a magpie. It's mother-of-pearl. I wonder why they never say father-of-pearl. We had a neighbour once, Pearl, awful she was, never fancied the name after."

"He doesn't look like a magpie," said the milkman watching Chatty try to grab the needle-box again, rolling dangerously sideways in all his woolly layers, "more like an egg."

"He favours his father," said Ma Grudgely. "There's a lot of that sort of thing in that family. His uncle was a chandelier-maker. It's in the blood."

"Nice little thing," said the milkman, but he didn't mean Chatty, he meant the box. He opened it and tipped it about. There was a little tray inside where the needles and pins lay. Underneath there was a mussy mess of cottony bits and a bunch of small gold safety-pins. The milkman emptied them out and arranged them like train trucks all along the work-top. Chatty began to scream with desire and had to be removed and strapped into his plastic buggy.

"If you're right," said the milkman, "that they're going, we'll lose a good doctor next door. Doctors can't just go like that. They have to make arrangements." He dipped his spoon in the Cat and tidily replaced its head.

"Well, they'd never tell *me*," said Ma Grudgely. "Not until it was all settled. They wouldn't want to risk losing me until just before they went. I don't know how they'd get on without me," she said, breaking a saucer. "Just an odd one. Very old. I never cared for gold and flowers," and she pushed the pieces out of Chatty's reach.

The milkman began to link up all the little safety-pins, slotting them into each other like a daisy chain. "You don't see these little things so often now," he said, "what with plastic zips and throw-out clothes. I remember our sister making chains out of them this way and our mother beside her, darning. Don't see much of darning neither, with nylon socks. Are we washing up, Mrs G., you not coming back till next week?"

"No, I like to leave it all to the end," said Mrs Grudgely. "I'll just feed the fish. Looks as though Chatty's dropped his biscuit in. It won't hurt them. Strong things fish. I'll leave you to close up then, milkman. I'd like to get to the shops."

The milkman took the tea mugs to the sink and checked the taps and shut the window. He found he couldn't bear the soggy biscuit floating on the fish-tank so he scooped it out with a soup ladle and turned the ladle upside down to dry. He looked round for the needle-box to put it in a safe place, but it seemed to have disappeared.

"Within," vibrated the Cat after the front door had shut. Sigger jumped and the fish gave a splash of surprise. She stared out through the water of the fish-tank at the feet of the Cat.

"Within?"

"Something wrong Within," said the Cat. But he would say no more.

The following week there was no change. Nobody had returned from Wales and Mrs Grudgely came and went. She did the washing-up and sniffed a lot. The garden was turning gold and there were fewer roses. The purple Michaelmas daisies were beginning.

One day the milkman stopped calling. Then Mrs Grudgely and Chatty began to stay away. Orange-red crab-apples shone on the trees and in the mornings a low white mist hid the grass. When it lifted it left everything shining and glittering and rich like a dream. The first gold leaves began to fall from the birches, leaving the trunks bright silver. The leaves fell softly on the dolls' house in the little wood. In the chimney the Trojan Regiment in its plastic bag thought sadly of the lost General.

Now, on Mrs Grudgely's final visit, the head of the Cat had been left lying on the work-top. Miss Bossy, who had been brought in from the outside sill on the sensible milk-man's last visit, was now leaning against his sugar-pot flank. A very tall doll, she was staring down at his sugary depths. Sigger had been delighted when she arrived. "It has been an *age*," she said, "I expect."

"Time is difficult," said Miss Bossy, frowning down.

"Oh Bossy," said Sigger, "I wish I were better at languages. Something very strange is going on. The cleaning lady was talking about it, but you know how it is. They talk so fast."

"The Cat understands. He hears more conversation than

41

us, living in the kitchen. If she'd only left him his head on he could tell us. I'm afraid it may be off now for keeps."

"I'm not sure how much he bothers to listen when it is on," said Sigger. "He's been very odd lately. I think he's ill."

"Ill? We don't get ill. We're not humans."

"They keep saying that the Cat looks almost human. 'He might be alive', they say. I understand when they say that. They say it so often."

"They're ridiculous," said Bossy, "I only hope the Cat *doesn't* listen. Human! What an insult."

"He isn't very well though. He keeps saying that something's wrong Within."

"He means 'Within the house' I expect. It's all upset and yet it's asleep. I know what he means. Life *is* wrong within at present."

"No, I think he means inside himself."

"It's this head-on, head-off, business," said Bossy and fixed her black gaze down into his interior. The inside slopes of the Cat were silky-white like the inside of a shell. Far below lay the sugar, for he was less than a third full. The surface of the sugar looked like a frozen lake. There was a little dark thing pricking up in the middle of it.

"What? What did you say, Miss Bossy?"

"Aha!"

"Bossy, look out! You'll fall in. What is it?"

"Ha! Ah! Aha!"

"Bossy, oh dear!"

Bossy had slipped so that her head now rested on the rim of the Cat's neck-crater. Down below her in the frozen mere she saw the sugar move. Then a tiny arm shot up. It was bearing a shield. It signalled frantically.

"Oh, oh, oh, oh, oh, oh, oh!" cried Miss Bossy who never got excited. "Oh wonderful! Oh!"

42

"Miss Bossy!"

"It's the General. At last, the General. Oh, oh, oh!"

"The Trojan soldier? No!"

"Yes. Yes. Trojan, Trojan!" cried Miss Bossy, and a face the size of a small nut inside its curling silver helmet was revealed. Miss Bossy's slipping forward had shifted the pot just far enough for the sugar to drift a little. Now an inch-long body clothed in the familiar armoured strips of silver could be seen.

"He's *there*!" she cried. "Sigger, he's most certainly there. But he's very still. As still as death. Though it can't of course be death. Oh, very still."

"Of course I'm still," shouted up the Trojan, and the echoes came bouncing round the china walls. "I've got my legs stuck up to the greaves in sugar. At least it's dry. Now, you'll remember it was a very different kettle of sardines on the Dardanian plains, B.C. 1200. Not to mention the first sack of Troy."

"Oh Trojan, I love you," called Sigger with tears of joy.

"Trojan, don't *talk*," cried Bossy.

"Oh Trojan, please *do*," said Sigger. "We've been so –" (She would have said bored, but felt it was unkind to the others.)

"Don't," said Bossy. "You'll start an avalanche. You sound like a loud-hailer. You'll crack the Cat. Can't you drag your legs out at all? Oh for a spoon."

"There's the ladle," said Sigger. "The milkman left it lying out to dry."

"We'd never be able to lift it," said Bossy, one eye in and the other eye out across the Cat's rim. "It's heavy as lead. It probably is lead. It's one of those great old-fashioned things, only good for show now."

Sigger was sitting close to the Cat's separated head, very

close to its foreign, green eyes. It occurred to her that the face looked so taut that in a moment it might split its glaze and turn to crazy-paving. The eyes caught at hers. They pierced right into her. She felt she was being barbecued or had become a button on the point of a needle. The Cat was trying to tell her something.

"The safety-pins," she said in a sleep-talker's voice. "Get the safety-pins. They will make a rope."

"But how could we get them over the Cat's side and down?" called Bossy.

"Hook them over your arm," intoned hypnotised Sigger. "Then raise your arm on its hinge. Keep it high. Move it sideways. Then lower it. The pin-chain will drop over into the pot."

"But how do we hook them?"

"I don't know," said Sigger, suddenly losing steam.

"And I don't know," said Bossy. "Oh dear, I simply don't know," and she dropped her wooden forehead, bump, on the cool rim.

"There is no way," came a wandering wailing sound from behind the dustbins, very faint, "all is over."

"That blessed Cry," said Bossy at once, lifting her wooden knob up again. "No fight in her. She deserves the dustbin place for ever. It suits her. Here, Sig, heave yourself away from the fish-tank and spread your arms. Now – can you reach the safety-pins?"

"And WHAT do they think they're doing?" asked the leading safety-pin over its shoulder to the one behind. It spoke in French of course. All sewing Creatures speak only in French. "What an undignified and ugly performance."

"For some reason I believe they are trying to reach us."

"How clumsy they are, these large and primitive species."

"I wish we had the needles here," said another safety-pin, further down the line. "They'd run the whole tribe through."

"I wish we had the scissors," said another, "to guillotine the lot of them."

"It's no good," said Sigger. "Oh dear – they're just beyond my finger-tips. We shall have to try at night when we can move more easily."

"Could you reach the broken saucer?" asked Bossy. "Try and shove them nearer with a sharp bit of that."

"This is an outrage," cried the leading safety-pin as the chain was jostled along and then swung towards Bossy's hanging hand. "I hope, *mes braves*, that you are properly attached? Clunk-click and so forth? The milkman is used to handling only bottles, and bottles of the most cumbersome kind. Neither scent nor wine."

"*Now*," said Bossy, "now, Sig. Push up my wrist-hinge. The chain is lying across the arm nicely. Drag it across and down the other side. Yes. Very good. No, don't knot it. It is twisted over excellently. Now we must rest."

They rested.

Sigger listened to the dripping noise of Cry behind the dustbins. It wasn't very encouraging. Nor were the Cat's eyes, a fraction from her own. She turned away her head. He was looking so gleamingly and electrically-whiskered that she rather feared he had gone mad and had confused her with a mouse. For Sigger looked like – But we shall come to what Sigger looked like later.

She lay thinking that Bossy had called her Sig, which is what people called her when they felt close to her. Bossy took her life very seriously, had great self-discipline and seldom got close to anyone. (There had been hints now and then of a very frightening childhood.)

And she had called her Sig.

The children – even the boys – had called her Sig sometimes, when first they had all gone to Wales for holidays together, long, long ago.

Soon the sun rose on the garden mists and Miss Bossy slowly raised her wooden arm. As the first rays of dawn struck through the kitchen window, she directed the arm at the air above the Cat's neck-hole. After an awful moment of nothing, the chain of fine gold safety-pins began to pour slowly, then quickly, down inside the crater. Bossy lowered her arm like a cox at a boat race and one end of the chain fell into the Cat and the rest of it down his cherry-bunch side and draggled its end along the work-top.

"Has it reached?" called Sigger. "Is it down to the sugar? Oh, I'm sure it's not long enough."

Bossy closed the eye that lay along the outer edge and examined the scene with the inner eye.

"Just about."

"Just about," called the Trojan soldier, madly waving his sword-arm and his shield-arm up and down and tangling himself in golden scaffolding. "Excellent! Nothing to it! Half a mo," and he wriggled himself and his weaponry inside the leading pin, resting his arms along one of the bars.

"Ready to be winched," he cried. "Heave away."

"Hum," said Bossy, "we'll have to be the judges of that. Not sure that Sigger has the pull. She's fallen flat on her face. The Cat of course is dismantled. Cry is behind the dustbin and the fish are no good at fishing. We could wait for the strength of night again of course."

"How much chain is there down your side of the Cat?" asked the Trojan.

46

"Oh plenty. Plenty. Down over the tail and trailing along."

"Could you weight it? Anchor it down with something? Then I could simply climb."

Bossy examined the terrain with her outside eye. "Difficult," she said.

"Imposssssssssssssible," came a long bleat from the dustbin.

Miss Bossy remembered that once she had been a Girl Guide. It had been in Mary's mother's time an age ago, but still: Once a Guide always a Guide. Hum.

"We need a heavy weight," she said.

"Hopeless," came the bleat.

And I'd like to drop it first on Cry's head, she thought. Then she had a second thought: that this was not a Guide-like thing to think.

"Ahum," she said, "well, there's the ladle. If we could somehow tip it over. It's very heavy but it's roundish. It looks rollable. Sig, have a go."

Sigger leaned against the ladle which after a while obligingly rolled over on to the tail-end of the golden chain, trapping the last six pins.

"Derailment," cried the final guard's-van pin.

"*Le débacle*," cried his neighbour and they all began to shriek and complain in their sharp French voices but too tiny for even Sigger to hear.

"Clumsy," they cried. "Anglo-Saxon. Ham-fisted. Inelegant. Embarrassing. Perfidious Albion. Give us back Calais," and so on.

The ladle held firm.

"Now," Bossy called down, "try climbing."

"Very difficult," called up the Trojan.

47

("Woe, woe," from the dustbin.)

"Very difficult and just what I like," the Trojan continued, and began the long twirling climb up the flimsy and hostile ladder. When he reached the Cat's neck he flung himself over, arms stretched and without a sound fell the great sheer drop to the Cat's tail. The golden, alien pins flashed past his brave eyes. He did not however see them. Brave eyes though they were, he kept them shut.

"He's down, he's down. He's with us again!" cried Sigger. "Oh *Soldier*!" and Miss Bossy slid slowly down the Cat's side onto her face, and lay still.

"I didn't know you'd made all this muddle-on," said Ma Grudgely to Chatty the next time she called. She removed the safety-pin dangle from the Cat's neck-hole and put the Cat's head on. "Now leave-over, for goodness' sake. We had enough you carrying that box-thing home in your hand. Reminds me, I never brought it back. Well, too late now. It's our last visit: All we've to do is take the fish to the pet shop and hand the keys to the Removals. This house won't see us more. Look, there's that little soldier-thing out of the bathroom."

She swept all the Creatures into a corner of the work-top with a greasy, cold dishcloth and continued to move the cloth lazily about as she looked out over the garden. "I'd best remind the Removals there's a dolls' house out there to take," she said. "Not that anyone's going to want it, the poor old wreck. Oh, all right then, *have* them pins. I'm sure there's nobody else after them. I'd like that Cat, I must say. I wonder if I could ask for it? They said I was to take a present. I suppose I can't have it and the television. And the toasted-sandwich-maker. And the electric rollers."

She looked at the Cat's face sharply as she turned away

and Chatty, who had been lifting a plump hand to pat it, and with luck knock the head off it again to get at the sugar, suddenly began to cry.

"Not that I'm sure I'd want it, anyway," she said. "It's got a funny look about it. The evil eye, I shouldn't wonder."

She left the house, slamming the door for the last time and went off down to her bus-stop. Chatty sat staring ahead of him from the plastic buggy. They were both hung about with parcels and filled with their own thoughts. Neither of them ever saw any of the Creatures ever again, though in years to come Chatty was to save every one of their lives.

4

Keeping Going

"And here in the dark we lie," said Miss Bossy.

Soon after Mrs Grudgely had left the house there had been a bang and a crash and a shouting. Big, rope-muscled men had come bowling into the kitchen carrying strong, light boxes with silver seams, and masses and masses of newspapers. "Kitchen first," they cried.

Within a few minutes cups, saucers, egg-cups, jam pots, plates, dishes, bowls, jugs, were being swirled up, each in two separate pieces of paper, and made into parcels. Like magic they were fitted together in the boxes, light as feathers, but firm. All day long the men worked. Saucepans, jam pans, electric-mixers, kettles. Teapots, bread-bins, wooden spoons, pudding-basins, lemon-squeezers. Rustle, rustle, chink, clink.

The men sang as they worked. They called about the house. Removals men are jolly people, rather like sweeps. Nobody knows why, except perhaps they like excitement.

"Finished this kitchen then, Les?" they cried.

"Over to you now, George."

Boxes were scooped up as they were filled and carried away, and the kitchen grew bare.

All still. All dead. You could tell that the cupboards were empty even with their doors closed. The air echoed.

"How 'bout the plants on the kitchen window?" called George. "How 'bout these milk bottles?"

"We was told 'everything'. 'Everything to go.'"

"Well, I don't know. Funny people. Think they'd be here to see to things."

"Artists," said George. "Bo'emians."

"Next door's no better. And they're doctors. They're on

53

the move too and nobody to say what's what. They've all stayed away. The doctor's gone. He's gone doctoring the other end."

"Other end?"

"Aye. Over there in Wales. And the artist's going to artist there, too."

"Two families moving together?"

"Yes, and not even relations. Neighbours here and neighbours there. Not usual."

"You'd have thought they'd have come back to say goodbye."

"Thought it'd upset the children. Changing homes. Bo'emian ideas."

"Maybe they all just got fed up with London. Didn't want to stop being on their holidays. Lucky for some. Have we to look in the garden?"

Henry looked in the garden and came in with a lawnmower. "There's nothing else much. An old, broken chicken-coop thing under the trees. They'll not be wanting that."

"No, there's limits," said George. "How's upstairs gone?"

"Very well. Nearly clear. How's next door?"

"Nearly clear, too. Both vans stacked full. Cup of tea? I've got a flask."

"Aye. We'll not use these milk dregs. Any sugar?"

"That's sugar on the work-top, standing with all those bits of junk. That big pot cat. We'd better pack that."

"Sugar?" said George.

"Aye – I've seen them before. Them pot cats. You take their heads off."

"That's not bad," said George, removing the head and putting it back several times. "I really fancy that. Nearly empty and no spoon. I could scrat some out with my fingers but my hands is dirty."

"Here's a pencil," said Henry, taking one from behind his ear. "That's funny. That cat closed its eyes at me."

"Softening of the brain," said Les. "One too many bits of furniture has dropped on it."

"I tell you it closed its eyes. It closed its eyes, disgusted."

"It's got a proud look," said Les, stirring his tea with the pencil and looking sideways at Henry. "Maybe it doesn't like sugar being scratched out of the inside of its toes."

"It wouldn't feel it," said George. "Its head's across the room. You don't feel things if your head's off."

"You do," said Les. "Look at people with their legs off. They say they can still feel their legs."

"Feelings stem from the head," said George. "The head has to be in place if you want to know what's what."

"Heard of a man once," said George, "perfectly sensible. Worked in an estate agent's. Died, and they found he hadn't a brain. Just an empty space."

"I daresay he had feelings."

"That cat's watching us anyway," said George, and he picked up the head and put it on the china shoulders. "Yes," he said, "I really fancy that cat," and he looked at it with longing.

"There's some would nick it," said Les.

But Removals men are very honest usually, and these three were usual.

"Now then, Les," said George, "we'd better pack it up. And this other junk beside it, I suppose. Last few." And he took off the Cat's head again and picked up Bossy, who took hold of Sigger's hand (for Sigger of course needed help) and they were both stuffed together inside the Cat. George picked up the little soldier and dropped him in on top of them. "Neat and tidy," he said, and looked round for a last twirl of paper to wrap the Cat up in, when the telephone rang. It sounded like ten telephones, echoing round and round the empty house and George answered it just as the rest of the Removals team came shouting and banging into the kitchen, so that he could hardly hear.

"We're there," they cried. "Come on. Let's get going. We've a long haul tomorrow."

"I'll look then," shouted George down the phone. "Aye, we'll look."

"It's them in Wales," he said, "them artists. They're on about have we got the dolls' house. There was no dolls' house, was there?"

"I've seen no dolls' house."

"Something about under the trees in the garden."

"There's that chicken-coop thing."

George and Les went into the garden. "Well, it *was* a dolls' house," said George, "I dare say. Once. When Adam and Eve was young. Come on then. Heave-ho." Between them they carried the dolls' house as far as the kitchen door. "How about these dustbins?"

"That I won't do," said Les. "Sorry. Not dustbins."

"There's something fallen down behind that one," said George. "Set this on the floor, lad." And he dropped his end of the dolls' house and rummaged about for Cry.

"Oh let be," said Les, jerking his end of the dolls' house higher.

"It's a rag doll of sorts," said George. "They're quite valuable, these."

"It's a terrible thing," said Les as George stretched for it, and Les let the dolls' house drop from his hands on the yard with a crash. The roof of the house which looked as attached as a roof could be – like a head – gave a sharp, snapping noise and fell open and back like a door, on two secret and excellent hinges.

"Now look what you've done," said Les.

"It's meant to do it," said George. "It's nicely made. You don't see work like that these days. See them lovely little hinges. You'd never know they was there. Look, it just lifts back. Not a crack showing. You could hide something for ever in there and nobody find it. Secret compartment. Can you fasten it down again?"

"Are you taking this cat, then?" came the voices from inside the kitchen. "Come on now, we're going. Where you putting the cat?"

"It can go in the dolls' house roof," said Henry. "Wrap it up and snug it round with papers. Safe as a stone. It'll not shift an inch. Best place for it."

They placed the Cat in the attic and fastened the roof of the house down over it. It fastened with a beautiful, silky click. You would never have dreamed that the dolls' house was not all of a piece. "Whoop-la, George," said Les, "dolls' house last. You're not taking that rag doll, are you?"

"Seems a shame to leave it," said George, and he fastened Cry in the front of his cab in the huge Removal van. She hung by the yellow trimming round her neck and the following day she swung there like a late autumn leaf, all the way to Wales. It was she, Small Cry, who led the procession across the City and on to the motorway, westward, then across bridges and rivers and mountains until they all reached the Atlantic shore.

"Oh, it's Cry," shouted Claire, hanging over the new Welsh gate, "look, look. Small Cry. She's up on the van. She looks terribly van-sick."

"She looks as if she's been hanged," said her brother, Paul.

"Me new mascot," said George. "Found behind the dustbins. I suppose you'll be wanting her back," and he unhooked her and draped her across the seaside gatepost of the white Welsh home.

"I hope you've brought the others," said Claire. "Sigger and Miss Bossy and the Cat and all the Trojan soldiers?"

"Did you bring the dolls' house?"

"That's there all right," said George. "First out the dolls' house is going to be, being last in. Here she comes."

"It's not our most beautiful possession," said Mary's mother as the rickety thing was carried to the garden. "It's very old and special, though. One day we really must have it properly done up. Here come the washing-machines and the dish-washer and the deep-freeze."

And it was weeks later that Claire and Mary and the two brothers thought of the Creatures.

"Something always gets lost in a move," said the doctor. "You will have to face it."

"The boys have stopped being interested in soldiers anyway," said the artist father.

"And it's not as if any of you ever actually play with dolls any more," said the nurse.

"I shall miss Miss Bossy," said Mary's mother. "She was mine first. And I loved the Cat. But I suppose we could easily go and buy another like him in Tenby. You can get one in any of the tourist shops."

"But I liked that *particular* Cat," said Mary, and in fact they never went to Tenby even to look.

For now that the two families were real inhabitants of Wales and not just holiday-people they never went into the souvenir shops. They left them for the summer visitors who had to go back to the towns again at the end of a fortnight.

Soon everyone forgot about the Cat. And the soldiers.

And Miss Bossy. And Sigger. Or at any rate the memory of them all became faint. The dolls' house lay beside the garden gate with Small Cry who had been tossed there sitting inside it all alone. The sand blew in from the beach in the autumn storms. It blew into the dolls' house until Cry thought she must be in the desert.

It blew in until it reached the sitting-room mantelpiece and blocked the stairs. "If I were a camel," she said after a year, "it might not be so bad."

"Or an Arabian princess," she said after another year or so. "Some hope for a Princess Cry."

The next year she said, "Or a palm tree. If I were a palm tree I'd be In My Element."

Outside the leathery seaside plants grew up around the dolls' house. The gold and silver lichens on the stone wall behind it spread across the roof with its sweet, secret catch under the eaves, that might never be found till the end of the world.

"I am only a Creature," said Sigger in a whisper.

"And here in the dark," said Miss Bossy beside her – inside the Cat, inside the newspaper, inside the roof, inside the Welsh seaside garden, inside the envelope of clouds and space that pockets up the world – "Here in the dark we lie."

"Ha," said the soldier after a number of minutes or years. "Ha."

"Yes?"

"I have edged my sword into the neck joint of the Cat. I am about to ease away the head."

"If that's all right," he added, "if it is acceptable."

"An anatomical hazard," said the Cat, "but I am used to it."

"It seems harsh," said Sigger.

"No, no," said the Cat. "It is what I am made for. But please do not break me. If I am to be anything I must be kept together."

The little weapon sawed away through the crack, cutting the newspaper beyond. "This is going to be a long do," said Miss Bossy. "We shall require all our self-discipline."

"We're all quite good at that," said Sigger. "We're not inexperienced in adventures."

"We've long ago got over any bothers with claustrophobia," said the Cat. "At least I have. It's worse for you three, down in my stomach."

Saw, saw, saw, went the sword. The soldier wiped his brow.

"Oh, I wish I could help," said Sigger. "It's frightful being armless."

"It makes you 'armless," said the soldier; but nobody laughed. It wasn't the year for jokes.

"I'll take a turn," said Miss Bossy. "Glory be, I should be able to wield a sword. I'm hinged like a suit of armour."

Saw, saw, she went round the wide circle of the Cat's neck. At last she said, "You know, I think I'm nearly round."

"I'd have said you were pretty flat."

"Don't," vibrated the Cat, purring inwardly into its stomachful of friends. "We aren't Claire and Mary. We don't have to make human children's jokes."

"It's not a joke," said Miss Bossy. "I am pretty flat. Or just flat. I'm not interested in pretty. That never came my way, and in all my years I never felt flatter. But the sword is almost round – "

Saw, saw, she went.

"Not in all my centuries – " she said.

"I didn't know you were into centuries," said the Trojan.

"When it comes to Time of course – " and he looked frightfully proud and distant (although nobody could see him of course because the Cat's stomach didn't have lights in it) and thought of the Great Siege of Troy.

"I have seen people hiding in stomachs before," he said, "and I dare say one day I'll tell you. Now the Great Trojan Horse – "

"Well, not now," said Miss Bossy (saw, saw). "I think it wobbled. Cat? Cat? Did your head wobble?"

"I think there was a tremor," vibrated the Cat. "Shall we say a slight heave? A little something above the left shoulder? Oh – now!"

Loosened nicely the head tipped away and musty air smelling of newspaper and dolls' house roof dust with a tang of the far-off sea, flowed in among the Creatures. Miss Bossy grabbed the neck-rim with her wooden hands and shoved herself upwards and out, leaning back for the soldier, who in turn scooped out Sigger. Bossy eased back the Cat's head, to make a thinking Cat of it again, and they all looked about them.

A very little light gleamed through the cracks of the dolls' house roof tiles, and the roof itself was stuffed with the remainders of the Removal men's paper which would need to be squashed into shape as carpets and wall-partitions if there were to be any home comforts. The space in the roof was not big enough for the large, recumbent Cat to be stood upright. So his long body would have to be shoved to one side to make any decent space for them all.

They listened.

Outside the darkness of their cell there was no sound of a household – no traffic, no hooters, no voices, no rattle and clatter of life.

"Listen harder," said Sigger, and they all stood still until, from far away there came a swishing, soft, sucking sound, very regular and determined. Very powerful.

"It's been going on all the time," said the Cat. "Ever since they took the house out of the van. It gets louder. Then it gets softer. It never quite reaches us. I think it is some sort of prowling animal."

"It will be the Devil," said Bossy. "I have heard it before."

"Or it may be God," said Sigger, who used to go with Mary to Church.

"No," said the Trojan, "no. It is called The Sea.

"I could tell you," he said, "Oh, what could I tell you? About the sea. The unstoppable sea. My great journey. My ten year journey. It might take ten years in the telling."

"That might be a very good idea," said Bossy. "It might be exactly what is needed. It might easily be ten years before we are discovered."

"Or more," said the Cat, "give or take an *annum*. I remember being entombed for two thousand of them, and most of those B.C., which was a very unsettled period."

"I remember journeys, too," said Sigger, "across the Alps on a finger-tip. Oh! What was that?"

"I remember, I remember," came a squeak from alongside the roof.

"Great Achilles' blisters!" cried the Trojan.

"I remember a very unhappy – "

"It's Cry!"

"Journey in a van. Hanged by the neck. Swinging over the Black Mountains. Boo hoo! I've climbed up from the fireplace."

"She's stuck in the chimney. That's where she is. She's out near the fresh air. Oh, how lucky she always is," said Sigger.

"She never thinks so, therefore she isn't. She doesn't think so now," said the General.

"She could be useful to us now, for the first time in her life," said Bossy. "She could attract attention. She could draw someone to us."

"I can't draw," wailed Cry, "I can't do anything. I never could. All I can do is mourn. I can always mourn."

"I went to a place once," said the Trojan, "where there was no morn. It was always afternoon," and he grew dreamy and sat down in a corner. He took off his helmet and sat stroking his silky hair. "Oh, the days," he said, "of golden story, legend brave and high romance."

"I'm so *bored*," said Small Cry.

"Listen," said Bossy, "it seems to me that there's one way only of getting through this next phase in the world's passing. It is the way we know best. The way it was always done when Creatures and Beings get stuck in a hole waiting for rescue, especially when no rescue will ever take place. We tell stories. We shall all tell a story."

"We never do anything else," said the Cat, "or at least you three are always at it. Not me, though. I keep my counsel."

"Well now you'll have to let it go," said Sigger firmly. "I think that Bossy's idea is the only solution. Our one hope of surviving sane. We are entering limbo, if not Eternity."

There was a wallowing, wet noise from the chimney. "Hope fading in that direction already," said the Cat. "Cry? Can you hear? We are going to tell stories."

"I have no story," said Cry.

"Mine is too vague," said Sigger.

"Well, listen then. Listeners are just as important as tellers. Stick your ear to the chimney stack."

"There's a plastic bag full of the Army in the way."

63

"My unit. My old Regiment," cried the Trojan. "Hurrah! Tell them to listen, too. Shall I kick off, Boss?"

"Yes."

"No," said Sigger, "I've been thinking. It seems to me that the Soldier's Tale will be the best. He is so used to telling his adventures. He's almost a professional. Oughtn't we to keep him to the end?"

"Oh," said the Cat. "Really? Do you think so. I see," and he lifted his eyebrow whiskers and twisted his Egyptian nose.

"Oh, I'm sorry, Cat. I didn't mean . . . You've never told us anything, you see. All I meant was that we should start with the dullest, which would be me, because it would be good to have things to look forward to."

"I don't suppose mine is going to be very inspiring," said Miss Bossy. "I'm only a plain woman. And I'm only wood."

"So was Noah's Ark," said Sigger, "and that always makes a good story. Look at me – well, you can't even look at me can you? I am only – "

"And I'm a nothing," bleated Cry through the chimney-breast. "I have no tale at all."

"Nor has a guinea pig."

"Well, that's a boring animal," said Cry.

"Absolute nonsense," said the Cat. "Guinea pig is quite delic – "

"Enough!" cried the soldier, leaping up. "Start with Bossy. She is our mother."

"*Am* I?" said Bossy, turning rose-red with joy and softening almost to beauty. She frowned deeply into the twilight of their stuffy prison for some time.

Then she said, "Very well then. Off we go."

5

The Dutch Doll's Tale

"There was once a poor boy, the son of a woodcutter, who lazed about the house all day dreaming dreams. He let the pot boil over to put out the fire. He let the wood stand out in the yard to get sopped through by the rain – and this was in Holland where wood is very precious because there are few trees. If his parents put him on to minding the cows he would let the cows wander about and drop into bogs, glug, glug, out of sight. Send him to gather eggs and more likely than not he would come weaving and slopping home with them along the canal, and Splash! Help! – 'Oh that idiot, he's done it again!'

"They thought he was a simpleton until he began one day to carve his father's faggots of wood, and then they saw he was a genius.

"This made them crosser than ever. 'Each to each and one to one,' said his father, a great glumping man. 'Wood-cutters' sons aren't artists,' and he hacked with his great axe and growled.

"'Whyever weren't you a girl?' said his mother. 'Then at least we could have set you to the washing.'

"The boy just smiled and went his way until one particularly ordinary day when the pot had boiled over and the wood in the yard was as wet as sump and the cows were all bellowing in the squelch and the canal had a coating of broken egg-shells like gigantic frog-spawn, the crunch came.

"The crunch was meant to happen to the stupid genius's head. It was meant to be caused by the leg of a table. The leg of the table was meant to crunch the head of the boy as it left the woodcutter's gigantic fist, the size of a good Dutch

67

cheese. 'Crack,' it was meant to go. 'Ow!' the boy was meant to say.

"For the boy had removed the loose table-leg while his parents had been tearing about trying to do something about the cold pot and the wet fire and the drowning cows and the cold-water omelettes in the canal. 'Oh dear,' he had said, 'I'm so sorry. Nothing much to be done I'm afraid,' as the parents had shrieked. Fiddling with the loose table-leg he had then removed it and begun to carve it into an extraordinary shape.

"Down came the table. On the table had stood three Dutch mugs of rich Dutch milk, three Dutch plates, all willow-patterned, showing an impossible, organised world, a big bowl of Dutch curd, and a fat Dutch cheese with red lino all over it. Everything went crashing and splashing to the floor. 'Roar,' went the father, 'Howl,' went the mother, and 'Lawks!' went the boy.

"And Wham, went the table-leg then as the boy ran across the yard – but missed him and fell at his feet.

"'Go!' cried the parents, 'and don't come back.'

"'All right,' said the boy, and picked up the table-leg and set off. He did not know where he was going, but that was quite usual. He whistled and smiled as he went along, observing the bowling clouds and the tidy fields and the cheerful windmills. He waved in friendly fashion at all the people he passed.

"At first these were only his neighbours and so they took no notice. 'There goes the goop,' they said. 'He's looking even a bit more what's-this than usual.'

"'Good with his hands, though.'

"'Oh yes – a genius.'

"'Genius?' said others. 'A genius from around here?' And they laughed.

"But after a while the boy saw new faces – dark, hard, miserable faces as he passed along. It was a dark, hard, miserable part of the country. Nobody spoke.

"The boy was not put off, but slept under stacks and begged for his food and smiled so brightly that the grim and bitter people set their dogs on him, and he had to run and run from them across the barren, water-logged countryside.

"He never minded much, but went his way as best he could, and when he rested he took the old kitchen knife that he always carried, and whittled away at the table-leg. He made small dolls from it. Quite a lot of them and gave them to the children he met. He was without the ability to think into the future, even as far as the next meal and so he did not sell them for money.

"After some time, perhaps a year or so, he found that he had grown very tired and very thin and that the weather was worsening again to winter. The rain never ceased, black rain sopping into the large black landscape. The windmills that had sparkled in Spring looked heavy and black.

"The boy had come by now to the Great Dyke that held off the sea from the whole country of Holland. He wandered exhaustedly along the footpath beside it and listened to the thunder of the ocean as it leaned and pressed against the other side of the dyke. He imagined the great waters, towering there above his head, held off only by the great earth wall. The rain was lashing over the wide flats of Holland, wetter, wetter, until they were as liquid as a brown rice-pudding. Birds skirling about high above the boy and the dyke, and able to comment on the view on either side of it, called out to each other that very soon there was going to be a spectacle.

"The boy had had a very bad time that day. He had smiled so much at the cottage doors when he begged for bread that the cottagers decided that he must be much less hungry than they were, and slammed their doors in his face. But he had tramped on. 'God bless you,' he had said. Now out of habit he said 'God bless you' to the dismal fields, 'God bless you' to the sea gulls who watched him above the dyke and thought: An amiable lad. Pity he never learned to swim.

"Then he saw the trickle.

"He saw, in the dyke, a trickle. It was a big damp patch, turning a lump of the dyke to putty, or to pudding mixture. Water was oozing from the bottom of this patch and making a greater ooze, the beginnings of a pond, a pond with already a stream leading out of it across the land. The beginnings of the crack that would turn Holland into a drowned country.

"'Oh, glory,' said the boy, and looked about him. It was a very lonely place. Nobody was in sight. Not a stick, nor a stone, not a tree, not a rock. All seemed air and water. The hole in the dyke was the size of a rabbit-hole.

"He looked at his arm, which was weedy. On the end of it was a wrist the size of one of his father's fingers and a hand like a bundle of strong but slender twigs. Nothing there to hold out the sea, whatever the legend says.

"'Nothing for it then,' he said, and took from his pocket the last piece of carving he had made from the table-leg, a tall and stalwart doll of not very obvious beauty. It had a generously sized head. And that doll, ahem, ahum – well actually –"

"No! Bossy! *Was* it?" cried Sigger.

"There was something of this sort once in Greece," said the soldier, "an ancient myth."

"I am unaware of such an event," said the Cat. "It is not to my knowledge part of Egyptian folklore. Or indeed

70

Welsh. Though King Arthur was very much involved with water, of course."

"Oh go on, go on," came the frail voice of Cry. "Do go on, Miss Bossy. I don't know any folklore. Folk never cared for me. Do please tell me, Bossy, what was it that kept out the sea? And how?"

Said Bossy:

"Now at this moment the boy had a sudden and connected thought, very rare for him and very fortunate for Holland. He looked at the size of my head and he looked at the hole in the dyke. Head-hole, he thought, head-dyke. Then, head-plug. And he stuffed me head-first into the hole and held me there, like somebody drowning kittens sideways. Though that was a thing he could never, never have done of course.

"There are many, many versions of what happened next and the most popular one is that the boy who saved the country of Holland from the sea was discovered dead with his finger still in the hole. This is nonsense. Another version is that there never was a boy or a threatened flood at all. This also is nonsense. Stories never start from nothing, especially when they pop up in different parts of the world at about the same time – or even at different times. There always has to be a grain of some sort of wheat to set them sprouting. And where the first grain of wheat came from, and who made it, only God knows."

"*Did* the boy die?" asked Cry, hopefully.

"Die fiddlesticks," said Bossy. "Not he. He stood there watching the storm and listening to the tumult of the waters on the other side of the wall and smiling kindly at any sign of life, even the bloodthirsty gulls – "

("Demons the lot of them," said the Cat.)

"And, 'God bless you' he said at length to a solitary

peasant who came tramping along in his sou'wester to see if the dyke was feeling well. The peasant, and then the whole of his village and then half Holland came running.

"They strengthened the dyke, first pulling my head out of it – I was severely discoloured for years. Then they carried the boy shoulder-high to the town and fed him with pounds and pounds of linoleum cheese and did clog-dances for him, and the King and Queen of all the Low Countries sent him a bag of money, and when the name of the national hero at length reached his parents, his mother flung her apron over her head with pride and his father went round shaking hands with anyone who was strong enough; and killed one of the rheumaticky cows for a feast and sent to say to his son, 'Hero and genius and sensible fellow, come home.'

"But the boy had no sort of wish to go home. He had rather a new wish, to see over the other side of the dyke. He took his bag of money, shipped off to England and once there he set about looking for a better knife.

"He landed on the breezy, lively coast of Kent, near Canterbury, and asked in the first town, in Dutch, for a carving knife. This didn't get him very far. The men of Kent were rather frightened. Through their keyholes however they told him that there were a lot of Dutchmen living in a town a little inland from the sea. They pointed in its direction and although he didn't know what they were saying he said, 'God bless you' and went there. And he felt very much at home there – as he would do still. That town is still full of Dutch houses – and he was understood.

"'Are you a butcher then?' asked the friendly Dutch-Englishmen. 'What is it that you want to carve?'

"'Just wood,' said the boy. 'But there doesn't seem to be much of it round here. It's not much better than home.'

"'Go inland to Canterbury,' they said, 'and you'll find a

great forest. And the beginnings of a great Cathedral, too. There's plenty of carving to be done there.'

"The boy bought a knife and went to Canterbury and sat about on doorsteps carving away at snickets of wood, and smiling at people and saying 'God bless you'. The men of Kent thought, here's a booby, poor soul. 'I should like work in the Cathedral,' the boy kept saying, and the men of Kent threw him apples. The great Master Masons of the Cathedral, looking as important as the Three Wise Men at least, pointed their noses towards the sky and the topmost tower and stepped over him as if he was wood-shavings.

"It didn't depress him. He sat carving away, bringing beautiful creatures out of ordinary lumps of wood. Soon they let him sit on the lowest step outside the Cathedral's West Door, and mermaids rose up out of curling waves of oak and elm, and sea-birds and fishes and windmills, farmers, and peasants and fishermen, old ladies and cows, and little ships with all their sails and rigging. All the things he had seen upon his journey came day by day to life. And he gave most of them away.

"But it was a very very long time before any of the Master Masons knew of his existence and it was one of the humblest and newest of the singing-boys who changed his fortune.

"The singing-boy had begged a mermaid as a present and had been so busy looking at it that he had forgotten to sing.

"'Confiscated,' roared the singing master – in Latin: languages were in a bran-tub in those days – 'Confiscatio!' and then – 'My goodness me! My goodness, gracious – !'

"A while later the Dutch boy who sat each day in the great porch of the Cathedral was being allowed to do the very smallest things in the parts of the Cathedral you can't see without a very tall step-ladder unless you are a visiting bird. After years he began to do the things you can see. After that, almost at once, the things he carved were the things that the pilgrims came especially to see and were in great danger of stroking them and gasping over them so much that they forgot to say their prayers.

"Now the boy was known as a genius. He became famous throughout the country and travelled all over it to other cathedrals and to cathedrals abroad. And when the cathedral people saw him coming, they took off their hats."

"And what about you?" asked Sigger.

"I was always there," said Bossy. "He always carried me with him. He never lost me. He never left me. I was with him at Canterbury, Selby, Lincoln, Ripon, and at last we reached the great glory of York. That's where we settled. We lived there until he died."

"And then?"

"Well, I've knocked about a bit these five hundred years," said Bossy. "I was made by a genius and sturdily for my master was after all a country boy. I lived forgotten and quietly in a Cloister for half the time. But then I got flung out at the time of some great disturbance. Some destructive king or other. Officials came and found me in my pleasant cupboard in the Chapter House and threw me out of a window on to a passing hay-wagon. 'Here's an idol,' they said. I fetched up on a farm in the grounds of an abbey ruin and I don't know how many generations of children played with me there. I went on and on, like the Abbey cats. Abbey-ruin cats you know are just the same families as the ones who ran about the old monks' kitchens. An Abbey-cat is not an alley-cat, you know. It knows its way around the Psalms. I am right, Cat, am I not?"

"I am not a Mediaevalist," said the Cat, "though I know a

thing or two about Christianity that the cats of your abbey never heard of. Just wait."

"I wasn't as free as the Abbey-cats of course," said Bossy. "On the farm I was just the strange old doll that sat on the high kitchen mantelpiece beside the horse-medicine and the tea-caddies with different kings and queens painted on them, and a very rackety clock. In the summer there were summer visitors at one time in my life and Mary's mother was one of them, when she was little. They gave me to her in the end. And now I am here, in a dolls' house roof."

"And you're still in good fettle, Bossy."

"I am not beautiful," said Bossy, "but I am well made."

"Remarkably fit woman," said the soldier.

"A very great survivor," said the Cat. "In my country, in Egypt, you would be accredited with reincarnation. There were quite a few of you in the Valley of the Kings. Quite a few of me, too, if it comes to that."

"Oh, Bossy," said Sigger, "what a wonderful life you have had. Did he ever carve anything like you again?"

"Most certainly not," said Bossy, shocked. "He was wholly concerned with sacred matters after he reached Canterbury. There is however – ahum, ahem – a wall-painting in the little abbey church at Easby. A number of Creatures living their lives in a very definite sort of way. Rather my style of limbs. I like to think perhaps I've had a little influence there. But like my master I am anonymous. It is one of the rules. We were quite unsung."

"I'll sing you," called Cry, and began a very slow and mournful noise in the chimney.

"Please! No!" Bossy's voice, always bossy, became for the first time in all the Creatures' life together quite shrill. "*Please*! Cry! Stop! I am a Cathedral Creature. I am used to plainsong of the very highest quality. The memory of it breaks my heart."

There was silence in the dolls' house roof then, as everyone thought of what a wonderful Creature Bossy was, and the amazing life she had had. And yet, to look at her, with her worn-away egg-shaped head and her staring black eyes and her mouth all pinched up as if she had been sucking lemons, to look at her, you would never guess. So smooth and silky and colourless she was, her old wooden body so faded but so complete, and so dignified her presence.

"I'm a bit of grey plastic pressed from a mould and there are tens of thousands like me," said the toy soldier to himself.

I am a pottery seaside souvenir, thought the Cat.

I'm a – thought Sigger. But it is still too soon to say what Sigger was.

"You are all very quiet," said Bossy.

"We are feeling of no account," said Sigger.

The other two said nothing.

"How ridiculous," said Bossy. "All three of you are sprung from the most powerful of roots. Use your silly heads. Everyone, everything, every Creature is interesting under the sun."

"But there is no sun in here," wept Cry.

"That doesn't mean it has gone out," said Bossy. "And the darkness is precisely the reason why we're telling stories. General, please. I believe it is your turn."

6
The Soldier's Tale

"Perhaps," said the Trojan soldier, after thinking a while, "perhaps, although I'm only a plastic cut-out, some of the spirit of the great adventures of the olden days is still hanging about me."

"Well of course it is," said Sigger.

"And I do seem to have some great memories. Hazy, but they're growing clearer. I think I remember – I *think* I remember a ship. It was a little ship with a curved sail like a kite. It was sailing towards me as I watched from a high place. It paused, it veered, it tacked. There were seven holes along each side of the prow, which was painted red. Four-teen oars came out of the holes and splashed the ship along. On the side of the prow was a huge painted eye.

"I was very young. Very new. This was to be my first battle. I knew the ship was full of soldiers from Greece. They had come to capture my city, the city of Troy. I knew I should have to kill them.

"The sea was dark as wine and the sun shone gold and the waves slapped against the tall sides of the little ship, foamy and merry. The soldiers crowding upon the decks all jumped out into the water. It was far away but I could see them springing about, shouting to each other and pointing to the shore. It did not look like a battle beginning, but a party. A splendid display. A day of festival. They were boys of my own age, you see, excited and happy at the thought of a fight. It should all be a game, I thought, I don't see why any of us should die because our Prince has run off with their Queen.

"I did not dare breathe such a terrible thought to anyone else of course. Certainly not to the soldier on either side of me in our hide-out. I was a professional soldier, in one of the crack units of Troy. We had been trained to be heroes, the beloved of the gods: taught not to fear death but to welcome it, to look forward to the crossing of the peaceful River Styx, the river of dying, and to arrive in the gentle country of the Shades, the after-life where we could all talk together about our battles until the end of time.

"The idea seemed very ridiculous that beautiful morning as the little ship was dragged up the beach. Other ships followed. A thousand little ships. Tents were set up. Fires were lighted. More and more it looked like the start of a carnival.

"Well, I suppose it won't be long, I thought, and at least I've discovered something about myself. Afterwards – if there is an afterwards and I'm not killed – I know now that I shall leave the army. I'll run away. I'll leave the defence of my country to those who are good at it. I'll travel the world alone and see if there's greater sense in any other country. With luck I'll be away before the Spring.

"My friends, it was ten Springs later that that fearful war was done. I was a boy no more, but a tired and sickened soldier. Up on the Trojan wall we had seen such horrors, week after week, year after year. The dead Greeks bleeding on the sand, lying for days unburied among the flies. Dead Trojans falling at my side. The stench of rotten wounds and bodies. The long sick weeks, even years, when nothing happened, when within the walls and outside them there seemed to be only death, and waiting for death.

"There were no plans. That was the horror. Our leaders never met. The Greek general, Achilles, for an age sat sullen in his tent. When at last he stirred – magnificently I give you that – he stood out upon the plain in all his jewelled armour and challenged our great leader, Hector, in a hand-to-hand fight. He killed Hector. We saw the great Prince fall, our

Prince who had seemed invincible, the Prince the gods had always loved. Achilles took his body and tied it to his chariot wheels and dragged it three times round the city walls.

"The war ended at last. It ended with the Horse. The Greeks built a huge horse of wood, out of sight of Troy city, and a queer, gawky thing it was, no more like a horse than you are, Cat. It stood there, crude and ominous, vast as a double-decker bus at the city gates.

"Word went round. Something tremendous had arrived in the dark. It was a messenger of the gods. At last, after great talk and disagreements we dragged it in and closed the gates behind it, and the citizens of Troy, such as were left of them, and the soldiers, such as were left of us, for those not killed or wounded by now had often died of sickness and hunger, the citizens and soldiers all walked round and round it.

"I watched from a distance. It did not look a messenger of the gods to me. There was nothing magic about it, or godly. It looked sinister, gimcrack, an evil joke.

"In the dark of that following night the Greek soldiers who were hidden inside the horse's body dropped out of its wooden stomach one by one, to the ground, at last standing on the soil of Troy city, and in the bloody battle that followed they slew enough of us to leave Troy dead. They set fire to beautiful Troy, and Cassandra, our old Queen, stood upon the burning walls and called out to heaven:

> 'Into the smoke she goeth,
> And her name no man knoweth,
> And the wind is westward, westward –
> Oh, Troy is gone for ever.'

"Through the smoke I stumbled weeping, unbelieving that Troy was gone and we had lost the long, long war. Most of my companions and all my family were dead and as soon

81

as I was found by the enemy I should be killed, too. There would be no safe corner in the land.

"I thought of the little ships arriving long ago, the enemy all so fair and joyful, the sort of boys I'd like to have had as friends, and I found myself down upon the beach, wading into the water, up to my neck in the warm sea, swimming then, and dragging myself up into the hold of an enemy ship. Some god – some enlightened, unwarlike god – must have guided me to the safest place of all, for nobody would look for a Trojan soldier in the heart of the enemy fleet.

"I lay curled in the corner of the bilges and must have slept. I woke who knows how long after, still with a sadness on me like an anchor round my neck, and famished and thirsty. After what may have been days of hearing the shouting and crashing of the sailors and the noise of the soldiers dropping the plunder of Troy all about I felt the movement of the ship change from the rock of the slow, harbour waves and become the lift and slap of the open sea. Into this sea I knew, when I was discovered, I would certainly be thrown.

"And so at last, I stirred. Exhausted, stiff and starving I dragged myself through the bilges and on deck – to find myself given food, and flung a tunic. Most of the ship's company looked little better than I did.

"They scarcely spoke to me, and I said nothing. But when they spoke among themselves I understood them – for after all, we were all Greek. Trojans are only Greeks under different names. It was not a crew I was with, but a company of survivors, raggle-taggle, tired, spent, unknown to each other. They had been gathered together by an officer – a huge, fine-looking man with a loud voice and an emotional manner. He looked no ordinary man. He looked the sort of man whom ordinary things passed by.

"His name was Odysseus.

"And so I became, my friends, a crew-man on a Greek ship, and very well-pleased to be one. But I would have been less pleased had I known at that strange, free moment when the sail of the ship filled with the east wind and we turned towards Ithaca, that ten more years would pass before I found a home."

"Odysseus was a great hero," said Bossy. "Everyone knows of him. But long before my time."
"It was long after mine," said the Cat.
"*I* never heard of him," complained Cry from outside.
"Tell us please," said Sigger.

"Well," said the soldier, "it began badly. We set out in a little company of other returning ships with a fair wind blowing, sweet-scented and strong and direct for Ithaca, and then, if you can believe it, I found that Odysseus had not had enough of battles!

"We attacked a city, the city of Ismarus, but we were beaten back by the Cicones. All of us began to worry about our Captain then, and when we were blown to a beautiful, sleepy shore, thick with flowers – flowers you could eat, and they made you drowsy and happy and unable to do anything busy ever again, and certainly unable to fight – when we reached this land of the Lotus-Eaters we didn't want to leave it. Everywhere you looked on this island it was sleepy afternoon. The great soft heavy-headed lotus grew on the rocks, over the paths, over the mountains, and like heavy curtains across the mouths of the caves. Anyone who tasted these flowers forgot their homeland. It was restful there. We said, 'You go on, Odysseus. We need a little peace.'

"But then we saw that Odysseus had strength. He roared at us. He beat us. He drove us back on to the ships, and slowly we recovered our senses. We showed him great respect after this and all went well until the Argos landed in the country of the one-eyed giants where one of them trapped us in his cave.

"You never saw a giant like Polyphemus. In fact we hardly saw him ourselves. His head was away up in the shadows of his cave and at intervals, down came his hand, feeling about for us and picking us up. He ate us like chocolates. We lost a great number of men in this way in the course of a single night. Only after Odysseus had made the giant drunk with strong wine could those who were left creep out from under the boulders in the cave, and then, while the giant snored, Odysseus put out his eye with a great pole and blinded him.

"In the morning, when Polyphemus had to let out his sheep who were sheltering in the cave with us, he could not see if there were any of us left, and he felt about, and felt about, with his great umbrella-sized hands, paddling and prodding in the wool of the sheep as they passed out of the cave into the sun. But Odysseus had told us to cling on tight to the underneaths of the sheep and hang on there, and though they bleated a lot the giant never found us.

"And so we escaped.

"There were great storms after this. They say that the giant was the son of Poseidon, the god of the sea, and had called upon him to make the sea our enemy. And our enemy it stayed.

"But we rested at last on the lovely island of Aeolia and there the King of the Winds took care of us. He pitied our little company and tied every wind in the world up in a goat-skin bag which Odysseus put me in charge of and I guarded fiercely. The rest of the crew became jealous – I had become a friend of Odysseus by now – and said among each other, 'There is a treasure in the bag. Odysseus has given it all to the silent one.' For I was a sombre fellow in those days and said very little in case I gave away by my accent that I was a Trojan.

"One night the crew attacked me and held me down as they opened the bag, even though I forgot about being discovered and screamed and shouted for them to stop. Then all the winds of the world sprang loose together, and the ships were blown all the way back to Aeolia again.

"Later – I'm skipping: you'll get weary – later we were in trouble with more giants. These were cannibals. As we landed on their island they attacked us, followed us back down to the sea's edge, and as we scrambled for the little ships, they hurled great boulders and rocks at us. And these cannibals sank every ship except ours.

"And then we were alone.

"We sailed on and came to the island of Aeaea, where the terrible sorceress, Circe, lived. She cared for us and gave us food, but she put into it a powerful drug which again made us forget where we were going, and all thoughts of getting home. She was a witch. She waved her magic wand over us and she turned us into pigs."

"You were *never* a pig!" exclaimed the Cat.

"Ssssh," warned Bossy.

"We had some sweet pigs in the dolls' house once," said Sigger. "That time the boys made the best bedroom into a farm."

"I, as it happened," said the soldier, "escaped becoming a pig. I was talking to Odysseus at the time. Trying to reason with him, for my influence over him was growing a little. Nevertheless it did no good. He had fallen in love with Circe, you see. I saw no future for him with her –

especially as he was very fond of his wife who was waiting at home."

"The witch might have changed him into anything – and you, too, Soldier. This Odysseus," said the Cat, "does not sound of great intelligence."

"He varied," said the soldier. "Intelligence becomes subdued when someone like Circe is about. She was very pretty. And she was in love with him, too. She doted. She clung."

"Like Claire's cloth she used to suck," said Bossy. "I was very relieved when she fell out of love with that. Very babyish."

"Oh, Circe was nothing like a sucky cloth," said the soldier. "She was a glorious beauty, and entertaining with it. But up to no good. I had to get hold of a special herb from the god, Hermes, to protect Odysseus from her. But even that did little good. He stopped wanting protection and settled down with her for a whole year. And I watched him smiling and smiling at her and lazing about, and her glittering back at him with her spell-binding eyes. And the ship asleep, warping and growing barnacles in the harbour and all the ex-pigs playing dice, and bored to death.

"When I at last got him free from her however, he had learned something. Quite soon after we had left we found that we had to pass some famous islands where there were stranger and more beautiful creatures even than Circe. These were half women and half birds and as you passed near to their shore you could hear them singing. Anyone, it was said, who heard their song was forever lost. Lured to their death. They were called the Sirens and sailors hearing them jumped off the ships and swam like mad until they were smashed to pieces on the rocks.

"Odysseus sat thinking long and hard about this next part

of the voyage and in the end he instructed every one of us to fill our ears with wax. Next he instructed me to tie him to the mast, and – you can imagine – to make a very thorough job of it. Any of us who removed the wax he instructed me to kill.

"And so we set sail, and my, how Odysseus struggled as we reached the Sirens' shore. It must have been the most wonderful music. I longed to take out my ear-plugs, but somehow not one of us did. I suppose the discipline of the war had been good for something. We all sailed safely past – though of all our adventures and escapes it is my not hearing the Sirens' song I most regret."

"It does all rather sound," said Bossy, "like the games the children used to play."

"Sometimes," said the Cat, "I rather feel that most things in History come back to that."

"But such a happy ending," said Sigger. "After escaping the Sirens you sailed safe home at last."

"Oh, but we'd hardly begun," said the soldier. "Could you do with a rest?"

"Whatever is happening now?" asked Bossy. The dolls' house was being lifted high in the air and was bouncing along to the sound of several voices. "In here'll be best. The little shed. It's dry, and a lock to the door." "Hardly worth stealing." "Sentimental value."

The house was set down and the feet and voices died away.

"Did you catch any of that?" asked Bossy. "I'm forgetting my human languages. We hear so little of them now."

"I think we've been moved indoors. There's a deeper silence."

"We're in for some more static, lonely years," said the Cat.

"I am of course used to it. Cats need people much less than most animals and Creatures."

"They're lucky," said Bossy. "I need people very much. And as for –"

"I miss people," came a cry from Cry, "though they never miss me. I miss everything. I'm a born misser."

"You're always asking to be loved," said the Cat. "It's a big mistake."

"Sometimes," said Sigger, "it is necessary," and everybody looked uncomfortable.

"Are you quite well, Sigger?" asked Bossy.

"Oh quite well thank you." But her voice – you will have noticed how silent she has become – was a thread.

"I'm sure it will be all right you know, Sigger," said Bossy. "It always has been."

"Yes," said Sigger in a whisper, "but in the end – There have been so many gone."

"If I could see you," said Bossy, "if only it were not so dark." And all the Creatures lay brooding for a time, for only they in all the world knew Sigger's secret, her most probable end, a more terrible end than Odysseus or the soldier or anyone in a book or any human being ever has to face, and much worse than death.

"Fate," cried Cry, "oh, Fate!"

"I think that the General," said the Cat – he was precise about titles and by being so pulled everyone together a little – "I think that the General should go on with *The Odyssey*."

"What I like about *The Odyssey*," said Bossy, "is that it has nothing to do with Fate. It's to do with character. Fate throws things at you and you have to decide how to catch them. I can't help liking your Odysseus, Soldier. He's so very silly and weak and he left his poor wife far too long awaiting him – there must have been quicker ways home than Circe's island – but he was such an inventor. Such a hopeful person. And so brave. Right to the end."

"So you know it?" said the soldier, after an embarrassed pause. "I see. You've heard it all before. I'm sorry. I apologise for boring you."

"Don't be a fool, General," said the Cat, "of course we know it. Everyone knows it. They've heard bits of it somewhere anyway. They know it in their hearts. It's one of the great stories of the world. But it's lovely to hear it again. Stories are for telling. And gracious me – you were actually there!"

"Well," said the soldier, looking still insulted.

"Oh do go *on*," said Bossy. "Tell us what happened next."

"The ship sailed next," said the soldier after a time, grumpily at first and then more excitedly as he began to re-remember, "through the narrow straits of Scylla and Charybdis at the edge of the Mediterranean Sea. Scylla was a terrible monster with twelve feet and six heads and each head had three rows of sharp teeth. Charybdis was a gigantic whirlpool. Anyone who was swirled into it was never seen again. Odysseus decided on one furious dash, telling us to keep our eyes front and think of the gods and the green fields of home. And woosh! Alas for six of us – Scylla plucked them off the deck like plums from a tree – but the rest of us swept safely through, and we slid sweetly on rejoicing until we came to another island.

"Now on this island there were silky plump cows and they were the property of the Sun-god and a very pleasant time they had, waving their heads from side to side and yawning and flicking their tails in the juicy grasses. We knew they were the Sun-god's cows but we were hungry, and so – I'm afraid – "

"What?" asked Cry, the simpleton.

"I'm afraid I know," said Sigger faintly.

"Yorkshire pudding and mustard," said Bossy.

"Yes," said the soldier. "I never thought it was as great a crime as some of the things we did, but it infuriated the Sun-god and he called on Zeus, the father of all the gods, to punish us. When we put to sea again we were sucked back, and back, and back until we were again by the terrible whirlpool. And this time Charybdis got us. It opened its flooded mouth on us and the little ship swooped down the terrible corkscrew of its throat. And in one second our beautiful craft was gone."

"But someone survived, soldier. You are here."

"Odysseus survived. I survived. That is all. As Charybdis grabbed the ship Odysseus grabbed the overhanging branch of a fig tree growing out of a rock and with his other hand he grabbed me by the hair. Later we clung to the ship's shattered timbers and floated on the tide. What's that muffled sound?"

"It's just Cry," said the Cat. "When they moved us just now they jostled her in the chimney."

"I can't hear properly," said Cry. "I want to hear the next bit. It's going to be the end soon and I know it'll be lovely."

"Did you say *lovely*, Cry?"

"Yes, Bossy. Lovely."

Sigger whispered frailly, "Cry, that's the first time I've ever heard you say anything was lovely. Except long ago your yellow-ribbon dress."

"If you could ease and heave yourself about a bit," vibrated the Cat to Cry, "just try. If you could loosen yourself from the chimney, you're quite near the secret hinge of the roof. You could just possibly wiggle your head through beside the hinge if you were brave."

"I'm not," said Cry.

"But if you were, Cry. Just think of the General and the whirlpool and the giant roaring and the feeling that he was about to be crunched up. If you just *were* brave for a moment, Cry, one day someone might come and find the dolls' house, and because your head would be inside the eaves and your body outside, they would know that there was a way in to the roof. They would feel about like the giant over the sheeps' backs and perhaps be cleverer and find the latch. And then, whoopla. We'd all be free."

"Oh I couldn't," said Cry. "Cowardice is my burden."

"Fling it off then," said the Cat. "Give yourself one great heave. Press with your feet."

Cry gave a half-hearted, dismal sort of push and found her head and the top half of her body high up out of the chimney. Tremblingly she bent forward and flopped down.

"My nose is in the eaves," she said. "I am looking inwards at where the swallows' nests would be if there were any swallows, alas."

"Put your hands under the ledge of the gutter. There's a long, quite decent-sized crack. Ease in your head."

"Ease in my *head*," wept Cry. "I'm not Odysseus. I'm not the General. I'm not Miss Bossy in that dreadful dyke. And it's airy out here and I can smell the sea. It'll be dark as pitch in there with you."

"Poor Cry," said Sigger. "It takes courage to push your head into the dark with other people."

Cry suddenly took a gulp and shoved. Her legs tumbled out of the chimney and she was left hanging, her head inside the dolls' house roof and the rest of her loose and swinging.

"Hello?" she called. "Hello? I've done it. I've launched myself into the dark."

"Oh well done, well done," everybody shouted.

"You're like Claire all those years ago," said Bossy.

"I hope it will serve some purpose," said Cry. "That's all I hope. My legs are a couple of pendulums."

"Penduli," said the General.

"But of course it will," said the Cat. "You may well be the one who saves us all, Cry. And while we are waiting I suggest we get on with the happy bit of the General's story."

"So then, over the glorious wine-dark sea," declaimed the soldier (he was just beginning to over-do it), "drifting on our broken planks, Odysseus and I at last came to the most beautiful island of all where there lived a lovely goddess called Calypso, and of course the old man – for he was old by now, my captain – fell in love all over again.

"Oh, he wanted to go home. No doubt about it. He told me so again and again and I urged him to again and again, for he had told me of his wife, Penelope the faithful, who was also clever and good-looking. He knew how she must still be waiting, if she had not died after so very long. And yet here was Calypso and she was binding him by magic to her side.

"Now this next event I like. It was not me and it was just this once not Odysseus's strength of character. And it was not the softening of Calypso that let him go in the end. It was the gods themselves. 'Odysseus has done his best,' they said, and ordered her to release him. Just now and then this happens.

"Calypso sadly helped him build a raft, and we sailed away, out of her safe harbour, though the god of the sea was still waiting. He tore the raft apart, and this time we thought we were finally lost. And *then* a sea-goddess called Ino – is anything wrong?"

"No," said Sigger, very faintly and after a pause, "no. It's just that I don't think I can stand much more. All in one life. All in one life. It's too much. And it seems to be darker here. I can't see – "

"It's plain sailing now," said the General. "Full tide. I'll speed it up. Not much more happens except the best and final thing."

"Hurry then," said Bossy anxiously from the shadows, "but be amusing. Hold Sigger's interest. Keep her alive."

"You know," said the Cat, speaking out sternly at last, "that none of us here is able to do that. And those who can are gone."

"I'm quite ready for it," said Sigger, just a whisper now, "but in case of the worst I want to say goodbye to you all now and tell you how much I love you, and I do want to know the end of *The Odyssey*."

"Forget the worst," said Bossy. "Believe nothing till it happens. The story is wonderful and should keep even a shadow alive. Soldier – quick march."

"Tossed on the green and purple ocean," cried the General, now going right over the top. "Flung by the mountainous cruel foam, Ino the sea-goddess took pity on us and gave us a magic veil which made us strong. Our raft again was shattered, but clutching the veil we were able to swim easily through hundred-foot waves and reach a friendly shore. And there we were given a boat to take Odysseus home.

"Now, for nineteen years the faithful wife Penelope had waited at home although everyone had started saying long ago that Odysseus was quite certainly dead and she must marry again. A great crowd of Princes had gathered together in Odysseus's palace eating his food and using his bedrooms and trying to be her new husband, and in the end she agreed to marry one of them when she had finished the huge piece of sewing she had been doing ever since her husband went off to war.

"So every day she stitched, and every night when everyone was snoring in bed, she pulled out most of what she had done, so that the last stitch came no nearer.

"But in the end the wicked Princes found her out and she had to agree to marry one of them; and she said that she would marry the man who could show the greatest strength and skill in a contest with Odysseus's great bow and arrow.

"The Princes, young and eager men who had had nothing else to do but practise, were hopeless – all of them.

"And then, into the palace hall there strode someone old and sea-stained and unrecognised (though a very old dog in a corner lifted his head and began slowly to wag his tail). The stranger picked up the great bow, and he shot the arrow which flew to the target like a homing bird. Then he slew the wicked Princes, every one.

"And then he turned to his wife. 'Now, guess,' he said. And she said then, at once, 'Odysseus.'

"And so he reclaimed his kingdom and gave me a place at his right hand and we all three lived happily ever afterwards.

"I think I'd like a rest now," he added. "I suppose even a Creature can now and again feel old. Or perhaps I am sad, remembering such amazing times. The sun. The ship running before the wind. Is everybody still there in the dark?"

"Yes, yes and yes," came from Bossy, the Cat and Cry, and "Yes" from Sigger like a leaf on the breeze.

"I'm worried now about Sigger," Bossy vibrated quietly to the Cat. "You must tell your story at once, Cat, and it must be a good one because somehow we have to keep her awake. If she sleeps, I think all might be over. Oh surely, surely someone will find us soon."

7

The
Tale of the
Cat

"What is a symbol?" asked the Cat, and at this absolutely terrible way of starting a story, Bossy and the General gave silent groans, Cry sniffed, and an even more ominous silence hung about the corner where sweet Sigger lay.

Then a soft, steady noise began to fill the dolls' house roof, a noise like a distant, good-tempered motor-bike. It was the Cat vibrating within (purring it's called sometimes), revving itself up for the tale to come. Lawks, thought Bossy, at this rate we'll all fall asleep and Sigger will become a hole in the air.

"I expect you can hear me," said the Cat at last. "Purring. They call it purring. Only the Cat purrs, but the Cat never purrs to itself. Do you ever go in to a room with a cat in it and find that the cat has been purring alone? No you do not. Cats never talk to themselves. The purr is to tell a cat's companions that it loves them."

The Creatures fell silent with self-consciousness. Could this really be the gleaming statue with the cold green eyes they had scarcely dared speak to in the London kitchen? Sigger murmured something grateful, though it was hard to tell what.

"Yes. Cats make few declarations of an emotional nature," said the Cat, "but this is one. What is a symbol?"

"A gold tin lid thing in a band," said the General at last.

"It goes whirr and pang, pang, pang," said Cry.

"Symbol, not cymbal," said the Cat. "I am a Symbol. Describe me."

"Well," said Bossy carefully, "you are almost the size of a real cat but you're empty and white. Painted with cherries and with a loose head."

"Not very nicely put," said the Cat, "but never mind for the moment. What about my feet?"

"I've almost forgotten – "

"So dark," said Cry. "We haven't seen you for years. Or it may be centuries. I remember the cherries."

"My feet have double claws," said the Cat. "Your eyes were never remarkable if you don't mind my saying so. Oh how I wish I could move my claws and scratch the chimney-end of this attic. Being a symbol is so constricting."

"I'll give the chimney-end a scratch if you like," said the General. "I still have my door-knocker. But why?"

"I'd like to get through to the rest of your regiment in the chimney."

"They'll survive," said the soldier. "They've survived Cry being in there with them since we left London which seems now as if it happened about the same time as the fall of Troy. Excellent discipline being inside a plastic bag down a chimney all these years. The longer they stay the bigger heroes they'll be. I dare say they might even get medals. They're regular soldiers and it suits their temperament, especially as they're Creatures and not breathing people." But he began to hack at the wall which was flimsy and in the end a mass of Trojan faces came in to view peering through the plastic bag.

"Such an advantage not having lungs like humans," said the soldier. "Odysseus used to remark on it in all our shipwrecks. I did much better than he did in the whirlpools. He often said that I must have had one parent who was a god."

"Good afternoon," said the Cat to the army. "Ahem. Now then, I am a symbol. The symbol of the ancient truth. The Cat you know at the very beginning of time was the symbol of the sun and moon."

"Whirr, pang, pang, pang," said Cry. (Either she was being really very dim or – could it be that she was changing through her bravery? Could it be she was learning to tease?)

"You mean," said Bossy loudly in case the Cat didn't know about teasing, "you mean that in ancient times, the first people in the world, when they wanted to draw the sun and moon drew a cat instead?"

"Something of that nature."

("Can't see why they couldn't just have drawn a sun and moon, it's easier," said a sergeant to a corporal in the plastic bag. "Silence," roared the General.)

"Something indeed of that nature. The Cat was the sun and the moon. It was darkness and light. It was the greatest end and the greatest good.

"Oh, I am immensely old. The Ancient Egyptians worshipped me as a god. When I died they wrapped beautiful ribbons and bandages round me and parcelled me up in a cat-shaped box and painted my face on it, and put me with hundreds of other dead cats on shelves in great cool pyramids and halls."

"Rather like a supermarket," said Bossy.

"Oh, I'd love to go round a supermarket again," said Cry. "D'you remember the old days when Claire and Mary used to sit in their mothers' baskets wagging their legs and the boys used to tear up and down and all the tins used to topple off. Oh Cat – they used to take us with them, Claire and Mary. We used to ride round like Queens of Sheba."

"You were not in the least," said the Cat. "I met Sheban cats. Very superior animals. You'd never get them anywhere near a supermarket."

(I am not only fading from memory, thought Sigger to herself, but I am going mad. And so are they all.)

"THE HOLINESS OF CATS," said the Cat, "before we get

completely taken up with the shopping habits of modern Europe – "

"Modern Europe," said the sergeant in the bag, "worse than anything in down-town Troy – "

"THE HOLINESS OF CATS became almost a religion in itself in Ancient Egypt, and as the centuries rolled along – the Sun-Cat never failing to rise by day and the Moon-Cat rising in regular patterns at night – the real flesh and blood cats of Egypt changed. And not for the better.

"You see, wherever they went they had become adored. They were bowed to as they walked down the street. They were fed like the princes of Egypt themselves. Sometimes they slept out their days on the lap of the King, the Pharaoh himself. On the very throne. The cats of the royal house were considered to be magic, to be gods, and when a new kitten was born, which was very often, there were the most amazing celebrations.

"Now this did the cats no good. No good at all. A cat, even an alley-cat, a scavenger over-the-wall-and-away-from-the-flying-boot cat, is very conceited naturally. Can you imagine what happens when everybody in the country agrees not only to let cats do exactly as they like, but to adore them for doing it? Yes. They change. That's what happens. They change."

"Cows in India haven't changed much," said a soldier in the chimney. "And they get worshipped. Saw them in the war. Your everyday Hindu worships them. Lets them walk around everywhere in the markets licking their tongues over all the veges. And all the people sitting under the stalls starving. I'd like to have given them a clobber, them cows, but then I'm not a Hindu, coming from Clitheroe." (The regiment in the bag was very mixed.)

"Maybe the sun-god was a Hindu," said the General thoughtfully.

"Nice quiet cows," said the sergeant, "peaceful-like. I'd nothing against them."

All became aware of the frosty silence that hung about the Cat.

"Cows," it said after a while, "cows are cows. They are not animals who are often on the make. My own species – of which I am a SYMBOL only, of course – my own species with all the very ridiculous adulation, slurp and slush of the Egyptian peoples who were at that time the most civilised people in the world (nations come and go) – my own species, the cat, in Egypt became a pain.

"The cats of Egypt grew so proud that their very faces changed. Their noses went up so high in the air – just go to a museum and see – so high in the air that they became arched like the nose of a camel or a Leicestershire sheep. The nose of the Egyptian cat went out to a snooty, arched point. The skull, observed from the side, became almost fish-shaped.

"And the eyes!" said the Cat. "The eyes. You know that the main weapon of the Cat is the eye. It is our STARE. Cats, after all, can even hypnotise each other. The eyes of the Royal Egyptian Cat became great golden jewels painted round with a sooty black line."

("That doll, Plum, was a bit conceited like that," whispered Sigger. Could it be that as Cry became more cheerful, Sigger the frail was becoming less perfect?)

"Our whiskers," said the Cat, "began in Egypt to shine like threads of wet liquorice. Our paws became flaps of silk, our claws blunted slips of ivory – for we had ceased to use them you see. Where is the point of hunting when all that one needs and more is served up, without our asking, three times a day and dead on time on platters of gold. Gigantic

Egyptian mice and rats could stroll about the temples, yawn and preen their whiskers in the larders and run across the black and crimson bed of the Pharaoh himself – and there was not a cat watching who could remember what to do.

"The years rolled on, and the fat cats ruled Egypt, and Egypt ceased to be the country of the bird-headed god, the lotus and the scarab beetle. Its great palaces crumbled and the tombs in the Valley of the Kings and Queens were robbed and blocked up with rubble. All about the three great dark pyramids at Giza, now softened and blunted at the edges by the passing of the years, sat the cats. A thousand cats. Ten thousand cats. When you come close to the pyramids, you know, you see that they are not straight sided. They go up to their point in giant zig-zag steps. And upon each zig and each zag there sat a large, self-important, snooty, fish-nosed cat, front legs straight, paws together, tip of tail neatly arranged over ankles, the tip not even showing a twitch of interest in the world. On some of the steps there was not one but a dozen of such awful animals.

"Our brains were addled, you see. Addled by praise.

"Now, there was one thing that still had the power to interest us, and that was the birth of the first royal kitten to the Chief Cat of the Pharaoh. The Chief Cat of the Pharaoh was still the special treasure of the Court, chosen with great ceremony by the Pharaoh himself – or so he thought, because of course people never really choose cats. Cats choose people, even if they are great kings. When the first people came into the world it wasn't very long before they went off and chose wild dogs to come indoors with them – but whoever would have been so optimistic as to think they could invite in a wild cat? It would have been like inviting in an electric storm.

"No – the early people of the world had to wait patiently

until one day after goodness knows how many million years, a cat or two on a cold night came and sat near the fire outside a cave. After another few million years, one or two began to wash themselves there. After another age or so, one looked up and nodded at the children, and a millenium later it nodded and began to purr. In the fulness or emptiness of time it at last put its head round somebody's door and suggested fish. Then cats were seen nonchalantly washing themselves at gateposts and then in gardens and at length changed their addresses and moved in to the seat nearest the fire. People don't choose cats, not even kings.

"Anyway, let me inform you all of the history of the squashy kitten."

"The *what* kitten?" said Bossy.

"Squashy."

"It doesn't sound very Ancient Egyptian," said the General. "They all looked so dry and flat. Like geometry, Egyptian drawings. Trojans used to laugh at the Egyptians."

"It wasn't," said the Cat, "it wasn't. That is just what the legend is about: The Legend of the Birth of the First Kitten to the Most Wonderful Cat of the King.

"Now.

"The cat of the king at the period I am talking about was a marvellous animal called Ptah. It had a golden coat and golden eyes and golden whiskers and was as fat as a sofa. It had been first kitten of most noble parents, who had themselves been the children of even more famous parents, Pubastum and Ru. Now for many months, since the election of the golden cat, Ptah, to the hot seat of the Pharaoh, the whole of Egypt had been awaiting the birth of the first kitten. An excellent husband had been found for Ptah (called Shu – a lot of cats seem to be called shoo) and everybody waited for the birth of their child.

"It took a long time. Usually cats don't keep you waiting. Ptah sat there eating Nile lobsters and looking smug. Shu yawned and examined his blunt fingernails. No kitten.

"Offerings were made to the moon.

"No kitten.

"Prayers were said in the temples.

"No kitten.

"The two cats were taken for long walks in the desert.

"No kitten.

"Egypt despaired.

"And then, at long, long last, it was observed that Ptah was looking smug and kitten-heavy, and after six weeks, away she went, as is the way of cats, to the King's best bedroom and got in among his finest clothes – and, hurrah! A kitten!

"But the first person to see it shrieked and fled.

"And the second person.

"And the third.

"And then the Pharaoh himself came with a procession, walking beneath a palm-leaf fan, his servants behind him all carrying saucers of milk, and his Lord High Chancellor last of all, carrying a golden necklace for the newcomer. The procession formed itself into a circle round the Pharaoh's chest-of-drawers and everybody looked down.

"There lay Ptah, stretched out taut and looking very strange. Her eyes were huge, like demented grapes. Her one kitten was feeding cheerfully and it looked like a peppermint toffee. Not even a newly unwrapped peppermint toffee. It looked like a peppermint toffee that had been chewed for a while and then spat out.

"It was a miserable, squashy, common little kitten, the sort you expect to find scratching itself and mewing and flea-ridden and far from home down in the coarse weeds beside a railway line or disused, oily canal.

"What was worse, despite the smeary-looking peppermint stripes, it was perfectly clear that the cat was going to be white. Now the white cat is the outsider. The white cat is the cat that disturbs dynasties. And it had the notorious double claws of the cat that never fits in.

"'It's very young of course,' said the Lord High Chancellor, wretchedly.

"But the Pharaoh strode silently off. Later he sent out a memo that the kitten would be given six weeks. In six weeks he would look at it again. In the meantime Ptah was to be given the best of diets to keep them both healthy.

"But Ptah didn't seem to want the best of diets. She seemed upset, distraught, unhinged. She looked with amazement at the squashy kitten and sometimes she loved it and sometimes she didn't. As for her wonderful husband, Shu, he seemed to have disappeared.

"But the kitten grew and throve and its stripes faded and its fur stood up in tufts all over it, and after six weeks, back came the Pharaoic procession again. Again it twisted itself up into a ring and the Pharaoh and all the nobs looked down. And the squashy kitten looked up cheerfully. And it was just as plain and common as ever. Its eyes were like pink shoe-buttons, and its face was good-natured almost to silliness. It rolled on its back revealing a pale pink stomach with spots on it and grinned at the Pharaoh between its large and peasant paws.

"'The thing's a simpleton,' said the Pharaoh. 'It's retarded. A throw-back. Rubbish. There's been some dreadful mistake. Fling it out. Get rid of it. This could never sit on a Pharaoh's lap.'

"So the Chancellor picked up the kitten by the loose bit

105

at the back of the neck and carried it from the Court. 'Get rid of it,' he said to the Captain of the Guard.

"'Get rid of it,' said the Captain to the Palace gate-keeper.

"'Get rid of it,' said the Palace gate-keeper to a passing pedlar.

"'Get rid of it,' said the pedlar to a beggar. He gave the beggar a coin, though a small one.

"'Bucket of water?' asked the beggar. 'Because if so I haven't a bucket.'

"'Just get rid of it anyhow,' said the pedlar, 'only make sure it's dead. It's something important. There's been some magic of some kind taking place. To do with the Pharaoh's cat. Somebody's stepped out of line.'

"'Stepped out of line, have they,' said the beggar. 'Well, I don't know. It's not a bad little thing. I've never been one to think white cats unlucky. Interesting double claws. Puss, puss. Kitty, kitty.'

"The squashy kitten gave a dab at the beggar's face with velvet paws and did a somersault or two to entertain him.

"'I don't like the thought of killing you,' said the beggar, and he plodded out of the gates of Giza and away into the desert. When he reached the place where there was still a scrubby sweep of green before him and the city still in sight behind, he set the squashy kitten down, and hurried back to his pitch beside the palace gate. After all it was a very small coin, he thought, I'm not really soppy.

"'All done?' asked the pedlar, passing by.

"'All done,' said the beggar.

"'All done?' asked the Captain of the Guard.

"'All done,' said the pedlar – and so on.

"'All done?' the kitten asked itself as it looked back at the wicked city. Then it turned and began to trot forward into the desert.

"On and on and on the squashy kitten went and the days were burning hot and the nights were bitter cold. On and on and on. The flowers at first appeared each morning at the rising of the sun, like a magic coloured carpet, withering and dying as they opened, but after some days there was only the sand, sweeping in all directions like a white soft sea.

"The kitten trotted on. It needed neither food nor drink and it never grew tired. It held its sensible stocky tail straight up behind it like a flag.

"A dot appeared, dancing in the desert, far away, and the kitten trotted on.

"The dot turned into a bouncing black cluster, and the kitten trotted on.

"The bouncing black cluster turned into a family of refugees, a father, mother and child – the mother riding a donkey, the child sometimes sitting up beside her, sometimes walking at the donkey's bridle. The father seemed exhausted and sad. 'There is something moving there, across the desert,' said the mother, 'some animal,' and the father gripped the long stick he carried, ready to strike. 'Where?' he cried. 'Jackal? Hyena?' 'No – some little wild thing. A funny ugly thing with a straight-up tail. It looks like a kitten, but it can't be.'

"The kitten trotted on, and the Christ-child ran towards it. 'It's not ugly,' he said, and held it tight.

"Is that all?" said Cry. "It's not a very long story. Is it true?"

"I've told you," said the Cat, "it is a legend. There are as many legends about cats as there are hairs on our fur. Except that I have no hairs on mine, being only a symbol from a pot shop. There are wonderful legends about the history of cats."

"Fairly *quiet* sort of story," said the General.

"I liked it, though," said Bossy. "Did you like it, Cry?"

"I didn't altogether understand it," said Cry, "but then – I don't understand much."

"You don't have to understand legends," said the Cat. "You are just meant to enjoy them – and be interested that they're there. That legend is a very old one (I've added bits to it – nothing like a few improvements). And so is another one that follows on, about Christ saving a cat from being stoned in the streets of Jerusalem and putting it in his garment. Jesus is said to have loved cats more than other Jews. The Jews are wanderers, you see. Cats do not choose them as a rule. Cats like a permanent fireplace. Jesus is supposed to have learned to like cats during his Egyptian childhood."

"You can't prove it. Any of it," said the soldier from Clitheroe in the chimney.

"Oh you can't *prove* it," said the Cat. "You can't prove Sigger. But she's there."

"Aren't you, Sigger?" called Bossy into the dark.

Everyone listened hard.

8

Rescue

Two men walked along a London street, one behind the other, thinking their thoughts.

The first one stopped suddenly and the second one went crashing in to him.

"Look out!" shouted the first one. "Steady on. You nearly sent me through the shop window. Don't I know you?"

"Sorry. No panic," said the second man, "nothing to fuss about. You stopped so suddenly that I thought you'd been shot. No – I don't think so."

"Yes, I do, you nut. I'm Tim," said the first man. "You're Paul."

"I'm Paul," said the second man, "but – hey! You're not *Tim*?"

They went in to a coffee shop.

"Well, fancy old Paul."

"Years and years," said Paul. "Good heavens, Tim. How's your sister?"

"Very well. Very married. Children. How's Claire?"

"Just like Claire. She doesn't change. Yes – married. Children."

"Ever go to Wales?"

"Not much. After you all left, Mother started renting out those cottages. Summer visitors. We should all go back there some time."

"We should," said Tim, looking at his watch.

"I'm seeing Claire next week," said Paul. "You married?"

"Oh yes. Married. Children."

"Me, too. Yes. We should all go. All of us. Children too."

"Well, one of these days," said Tim. "Pretty busy."

"Me, too. Yes. We should all go. Well, goodbye. I can't believe it. Old Tim."

"Old Paul."

Outside in the street they stood on the pavement near where they had crashed in to each other. They exchanged addresses, writing them down in notebooks, with a flourish. Tim went hurtling off, leaping through the traffic, waving his brief-case, looking happy. Paul turned back to look in the shop window to see what it was that had made Tim stop so suddenly.

The shop window was full of china cats.

"And I remember that biscuit-tin," said Mary on the beach in Wales. "It reminds me of the dolls' house door."

A huge number of people was on the beach: Mary and her family, Claire and her family, Paul and some of his family, Tim's family – Tim was coming later – Claire and Mary's mothers were there. They were now of course grannies. Mary's father, the painter, was dreaming about on some rocks. Claire's father was still doctoring. Still visiting ill people and saying don't panic. He would be coming later, too. "I'll be at the picnic all right," he'd said. "Nothing to worry about. Perfectly normal."

So it was a very big party of old friends and new relations on the beach and the grannies had their backs against the cliff, buttering away at buns, and talking. Claire and Mary had their eyes on the sea and the sea's edges where their children were splashing and swimming as far out as they could. Mary's little boy was trying to reach a raft but Claire's children were attacking him from either side. He had to get between them to reach the raft. "He's between Scylla and Charybdis," said Paul. "Do you remember the Trojan soldiers?"

"No," said Claire. "What Trojan soldiers?"

"I do," said Mary. "They had a hard time, getting dropped from the top of the dolls' house when you two boys took the stairs out. It was a wonderful dolls' house."

"I'll tell you something queer," said Claire and screamed at her children. Mary's child was being walloped by Scylla and Charybdis at once, and seemed to be sinking.

"Something queer. I went back to our old houses the other day."

"Which houses?"

"Well, the houses outside London. The houses where we had the dolls' house under the trees."

"It wasn't under trees. It was in a high attic, under a sort of shelf."

"No. Later on it was in a little wood. I found the two houses, side by side, but they'd grown much smaller. They were like dolls' houses themselves. And no trees at all at the bottom of the garden. Just a crowd of little new houses surrounded by concrete."

"I wouldn't have wanted to see. I remember a wonderful place."

"Yes. Well. Then I walked down the High Street."

"I don't remember a High Street. Oh yes – something. There was a little sweet-shop full of crowds of us and a shopkeeper shouting out, 'Only two in here at a time,' and slapping our hands to keep us off the sweet-bottles. She had a twitch. I think she died of worry."

"The sweet-shop's a boutique now. Full of awful clothes, hanging like dead birds. Well, then I went along the High Street and there was an antique shop and I went in and I saw something just inside on the desk. It was the needle-box."

"What needle-box?"

"Well, our *needle*-box. The dolls' house dolls' house. Don't you remember?"

"I say, we were barmy children, weren't we?" said Mary. "How could it have been? The same one?"

"I knew it. I knew it as if it was my own fingernails. It's a little black, lacquer box, an inch wide and two inches long and it's set with splinters of mother-of-pearl in the top."

"Oh yes. Yes, I remember. Well but – there must be hundreds like it."

"There aren't. I opened it. It's full of needles and pins. Our old needles and pins."

"Did you buy it?"

"I tried. That's what's so strange. He was a big fat silent sort of man. He sat glaring in the shadows. I picked up the needle-box and he said, 'Not for sale.' No 'Sorry'. No anything."

"'I'd give you – well, quite a lot of money,' I said.

"He came up and took it from me.

"'Not for sale. I'd not sell it,' he said. 'It's what I began with. Had it all my life.'

"'It's not really very valuable,' I said.

"'Matter of opinion,' he said. 'A keepsake. Had it when I was two.'

"'I wouldn't have thought a child of *two* – '

"'It's in the blood,' he said. 'You're born with a feeling for objects. It's like curly hair. My mother said it was when I was two years old. Brought me luck. Always been on my desk.'

"He had one of those big, still, faces. 'Grudgely' he was called. 'Chetwode Grudgely'. Not a name you can forget. It rang some sort of a bell. Perhaps he's on the telly."

"How funny – that little black box still in the same town. Maybe time doesn't move so fast after all."

The day was perfect. The beach was hazy and hot, and quiet because it was September and most of the holiday people had gone, since school had started again. Mary's and Claire's, Tim's and Paul's children were still too young for school. The grandmothers and mothers, the fathers and grandfathers, a scatter of friends, were all talking quietly, the older ladies in hats.

The picnic began. Bottles of home-made lemonade were diluted with fizzy water. Sandwiches were squashy and damp and tasted wonderful. Shortbread biscuits were handed round, and big tomatoes and some red apples. Sleepy wasps were waved away. The sea went swish and was then quite silent. Then it went swish, again. It dragged itself back over the hard, gold sand with a contented sigh. The pools were deep and clear.

The children lay on their stomachs trying to take the limpets on the rocks unawares and pull them from their refuge. Even the children talked quietly. Even the grannies. The great black cliffs loomed up behind and crocodile rocks lifted their noses out to sea. No cloud in all the sky.

"He didn't have the dolls' house in his shop?" said Claire. "I wonder where that went?"

"Oh, poor old thing. Fell to bits I expect. It'll be under the cement of the horrible new houses."

"No. It came with us out here to Wales. It came separately, didn't it? There was something . . . Didn't the dolls and the Creatures all sit up in the front of the removal van?"

"I remember something," said Mary. "It was shoved in the garden. It stood there for years. In the corner under the wall. With the yellow lichen."

"It would be frightfully valuable now. We were awful children, you know. We never looked after anything. We let those dolls rot away."

"It was our parents' fault. How were we to know it was valuable? It was just part of everything else."

"What was your parents' fault?" called Claire's father, who had now arrived. "What's the fuss now?"

"That dolls' house we once had. It must have been worth a bomb. It was a lovely old one with a wonderful big front door. The one I got stuck in."

"Yes. I always meant to do something about that. Do it up. We did make one sort of an attempt."

"It disappeared in the move," said Mary's mother.

"No it didn't," said Claire's mother. "Certainly not. It came to our cottage. After you all went away I had it moved into the stone wash-house at the end of the garden."

"Where did it go then?"

"It didn't go anywhere. I expect it's still there."

"I don't think I'd want to see it again," said Claire. "It would be such a reproach. And awfully sad. Without the dolls, and so on."

"You don't think – " said Mary. "I suppose the dolls and Creatures couldn't still be in it?"

"Of course not. They'd be dust and rags. Except of course for the invisible one."

Claire and Mary laughed.

"You don't think the invisible one's still alive then?"

"Well, scarcely. When did you last think of her, Claire?"

Mary's mother said, "We all got awfully tired of that invisible one. What was she called – Etty? Etter?"

"Litter," said Claire's father.

"No! She was *not* called litter," Mary and Claire said together.

"She was called – " But Mary couldn't remember. Her child by the sea had left the puddly place he was trying to dam against the tide and was tottering towards the crocodile

116

rocks. "He's not exactly the boy who saved Holland," said his mother. "Five minutes is enough for him. Hi!" The baby was going fast and the sea was making a growling noise as he approached. Mary went dashing away.

"Flicker. That's what it was," said Tim. "That was the name of your imaginary friend, Claire. Barmy."

"You all believed in her, though," said Claire's mother. "I think I rather believed in her. But I don't think it was 'Flicker'."

The sun was a little lower. The light was a little more gold. The grannies and aunts and grandfathers were beginning to press lids on biscuit-tins, and to shake and fold the rugs. The biscuit-tin that had once held peppermint snow-cakes still had its string of camels, now rather faded, walking with a mixture of disgust and pride across a pink and purple desert, three dark pyramids behind.

Claire thought most mystifyingly of jelly-sprats. "Sigger," she said, "Sigger was her name."

"Mary," she called out, "Mary" – she was rubbing her child with a towel and saying don't squeak; it's only sand. We have to get some of it off – "Mary – it was Sigger."

Mary, with the failed Dutch hero under her arm, came up and began to rub him with a towel, too. "Yes, Sigger," she said. "It's funny. When you say Sigger, what do you feel?"

Claire said, "I have to go in between the toes so stop yapping. Otherwise you'll never get your sandals on. 'Sigger'? – Well, I feel rather happy, for some reason."

They all walked in a raggedy procession off the beach and into the cars, tossing in the baskets, the sandy towels, the biscuit-tins, the spades. At the cottage Claire and Mary got out, hung around with their children. "Shall we look in the stone shed?" asked Claire.

"Oh, some time," said Mary. "Enough is enough. Let's get them to bed first." When the children were in bed, there was supper to cook. Tired with the sun the children slept. The parents ate sleepily, and talked. "Sigger," said Paul. "Do your kids have an imaginary friend, Tim?" "Oh yes," said Tim. "They say when you forget the name of your imaginary friends you're old," said Paul. "Some people don't have them," said Claire, "I wonder why?" "They don't choose to," said Mary, "but then, I never chose Sigger." "Sigger just appeared," said Claire, "very interesting really." "Maybe she chose us," said Mary. "Well, poor thing she's dead and gone now. She can't live without us." "We're talking about her still," said Claire, "and we've remembered her name."

Outside the sea sighed and splashed, the limpets took off from the rocks, the fish swam a little nearer the surface. Inland, mice ran pitter-patter over the dolls' house roof in the stone wash-house. Sigger said suddenly, very clearly, "Bossy? Cry? Bossy? Are you there?"

"Are you there, Sigger?"

"Cat?" called Sigger. "Cat?"

"Good evening, Sigger."

"General?"

"Service, Ma'am."

"Oh, my dear friends," said Sigger and was silent.

"It's only a remission," said Cry. "She's on the way. They often have lucid moments before death, these imaginary ones. Poor thing – terrible to be only a figment. A happy release – "

"Be quiet," said Bossy, "how dare you, Cry?" Had she not been made of an old table-leg, she knew that she would have wept. Indeed, even the Cat, had he not been a symbol of the

118

sun and moon and a relation of a kitten who had once met Jesus Christ, might have weakened, too. Suddenly the friend of Ulysses, the wily Odysseus, hero of the Trojan War, who had withstood the drunken one-eyed giant, the Sirens, and the terrible dragons of the sea – leaned against the chimney and began to make gulping noises. Even within earshot of his regiment he did not disguise them as the saddest of sobs.

The Cat, lying on its china side, said privately to Bossy, who was propped near his whiskers, "We must face it. She will be gone by morning."

The harvest moon rose over the Welsh cottage where a child called out in its sleep. At length Bossy answered the Cat. "Yes," she said, "I think you're right. But we won't forget her."

"How do we know?" asked Small Cry. "There's a deal even we must have forgotten, all these years." And for once nobody answered.

A door opened in the cottage and there was a sound of bare feet on flagstones and quiet voices. Claire and Mary carrying candles came walking towards the wash-house. Under one arm Mary carried a child. The door of the wash-house squealed and groaned.."Hush," said Claire, "we don't want all the children awake. Why couldn't we sleep?"

"Because this one wouldn't," said Mary, setting her baby on the floor where it made cheerful noises as if it were morning. Claire held her candle high.

"So much junk," she said. "We'd never see. No sign of a dolls' house. Piles of wood. Old pram. A rusty lawn-mower. A broken boat. A pair of legs."

"Pair of legs," said Mary, moving a heap of old cardboard boxes to see them better. "Goodness – legs! And in a yellow

dress made out of your old hair-ribbons. Claire, for goodness' sake! It's Cry! It's old misery-bags. Without her head.
The rats must have got it. No – it's stuck in something.
Look, she's got her head stuck somehow – under the eaves of
the dolls' house. The dolls' house is there."

"How could she get her head stuck in the eaves? The roof
didn't lift off, did it? We certainly didn't know that it did."

They put the baby in the old pram and the candles in the
holes in the wash-house wall where lamps had once stood
and began to move all the rubbish away from the dolls'
house door.

"Oh, look at it! Oh Mary, it's a most *wonderful* dolls'
house. We never knew. Oh, weren't we spoiled? Fancy
letting it get like this. It's an antique."

"Well, so long as Chetwode Grudgely doesn't get it."

Claire was feeling with her fingers under the roof eaves,
trying to free Cry's head. "There's a sort of catch here," she
said, prodding. "Oh! Oh goodness!"

The roof of the dolls' house sprang back on its secret
hinges like the lid of a pointed-topped box. Cry fell to the
ground with a martyred look and Mary picked her up. Claire
felt about inside. "Bring a candle quickly," she said, and
Mary gave Cry to the baby and lifted both candles towards
the dark corner.

"It's Bossy! Mary – good gracious, Bossy! And that lovely
Cat that used to be in the kitchen, full of sugar, and that
Trojan soldier I found in my hair and rescued from drowning in the bath. And look – there's a whole bagful of soldiers
looking at us, all stuck down the chimney!"

Mary took back Cry and sat her inside, too.

"D'you think Sigger's there?" she said.

"Well, of *course* she's there," said Claire. "Of *course* she's
there. None of us could survive without Sigger."

120

Mary's baby wanted to see in the roof too, so they picked her up and all three of them gazed; and suddenly, in the moonlight and candlelight of the shed, Sigger shone out for a moment like a star, brilliant and joyful.

They couldn't of course touch her or carry her in to the house, or sit her along the kitchen window-ledge in the cottage with the rest, ready for morning, but she was there with them just the same. Mary's baby wanted to take the Cat to bed with her but she wasn't allowed.

"Tomorrow we'll wash them all," said Mary, "and we'll make Cry a new dress. And we'll take the dolls' house to London and we'll turn it into a glorious mansion."

"We were always just about to do that," said Claire.

"And the dolls and the Creatures shall live happy ever after."

"All well?" asked Sigger strongly as the sun rose.

"Excellent," they all said, and sat smiling at the new day.

The End